T[
Portal of
Alesia

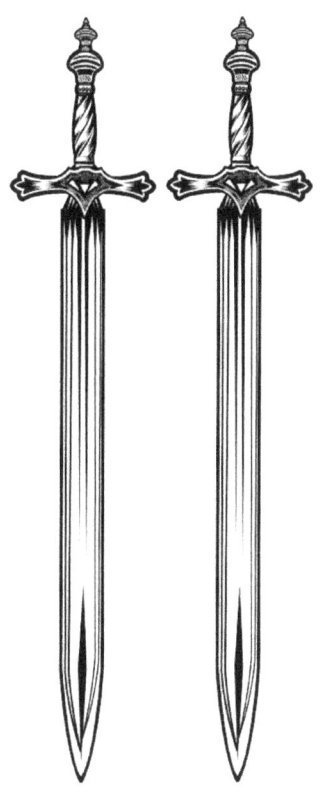

The Portal of Alesia

Book 2 of the Quester Trilogy

By
W. B. Speir

Names, characters, businesses, places, events, and incidents are either the products of the author's imagination or used in a fictitious manner. Any resemblance to actual persons, living or dead, or actual events, is purely coincidental.

No part of this publication may be reproduced, stored in a retrieval system, or transmitted in any form or by any means, electronic, mechanical, photocopying, recording, or otherwise, without the written permission of the publisher.

Text Copyright © 2024 W. B. Speir

All rights reserved.
Published 2024 by Progressive Rising Phoenix Press, LLC
www.progressiverisingphoenix.com

ISBN: 978-1-958640-56-2

Printed in the U.S.A.
1st Printing

Front Cover Photos: "Fantasy Beautiful Landscape With Magic Portal in Mystic Fairy Tale Forest" Stock Photo ID: 2192425231 By Bisams. Images used under license from Shutterstock.com.

Interior Illustration: "Legendary Sword." Stock Vector ID: 1711886083 By omnimoney. Image used under license from Shutterstock.com.

Cover design by William Speir

Book design by William Speir
Visit: http://www.williamspeir.com

I was raised by a narcissist who married a prince. My wonderful father chased her for 5 years, and they were married for 37 years until he passed. She lived another 20 years—bitter and controlling until her last breath. I survived by escaping from that environment, leaving behind both the good with the bad, and I made myself into what I am—a little sane, a little crazy, moderately successful, and basically very happy.

The love of my life and I crossed paths 26 years ago, and that relationship has made me a better person. We met in July and were married in November of the same year. With this wonderful person at my side, I became a parent, and I found the true meaning of love.

To those who say that true love is a lie, I beg to differ. I'm living proof that it is quite real... and extraordinarily wonderful. Never lose hope. Keep the faith.

Content Warning:

The Portal of Alicia is an adult Romantasy novel. The story includes elements that may not be suitable for all readers. In addition to depictions of violence and scenes of a strong sexual nature, this story contains a scene depicting the physical torture of one of the female characters, along with threats of sexual assault. Readers who may be sensitive to these depictions please take note.

TABLE OF CONTENTS:

THE TAVERN 1
    Chapter 1 2
THE QUEST BEGINS 13
    Chapter 2 14
    Chapter 3 28
    Chapter 4 45
    Chapter 5 59
    Chapter 6 73
    Chapter 7 90
    Chapter 8 106
    Chapter 9 120
    Chapter 10 136
    Chapter 11 148
    Chapter 12 162
    Chapter 13 180
RETURNING HOME 193
    Chapter 14 194

The Tavern

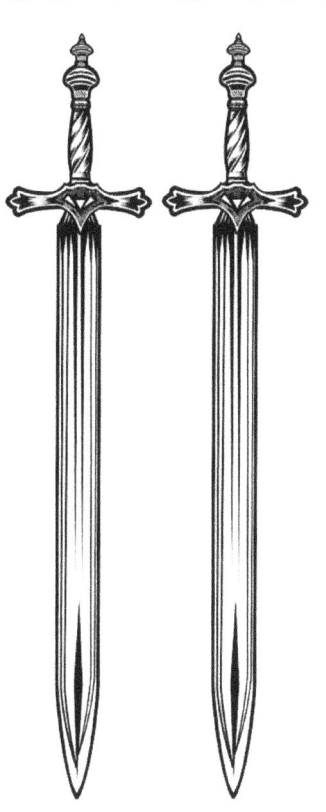

Chapter 1

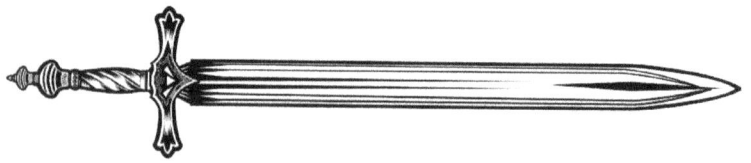

Nikki and her teammates found themselves standing in the tavern again, but something was different this time. There was a large wooden bar on the doors, and the shutters had been closed and locked.

Nichole "Nikki" Frasier, Justin Bradford, Bethany Parrott, Thor Larkin, Allison Maccabe, Peter Jordan, Olivia "Livvy" Bainbridge, and Kevin Dunross were all wearing the same outfits and weapons they wore on their last quest. Everything seemed the same, but Nikki was certain that something different was going on.

"Greetings courageous questers," the tavern owner said gravely. "I'm grateful you're here. We need your help... I need your help."

The tavern owner poured everyone a tankard of mead.

"Why are the doors locked?" Justin asked.

"The tavern is closed until this evening," the tavern owner stated, taking a drink from his own tankard. "There are things I need to tell you that cannot be overheard, and it all relates to the quest I need you to accept."

The tavern owner motioned for everyone to drink, then he continued. "First, I need to clear up a few misconceptions I know you have from your first quest. You are *not* inside of a game, and you are also no longer on your world. This world is known as Annwyn, and you will find that name in your own world's mythology. That's because there has been a link between our worlds for eons. In fact, your world helped to populate my world. But I'm getting ahead of myself."

The tavern owner led the questers to one of the empty tables. Fresh bread and roasted meats were served, tankards were refilled, and then the tavern owner's assistants disappeared into the storeroom behind the bar.

"So this is a real place?" Thor asked.

The tavern owner nodded. "As real as your own world. Our civilization has existed for almost as long as yours. The difference is: we saw no reason to advance our technology, but you did."

"Why?" Livvy asked.

"Magic, I guess," the tavern owner replied. "Your people replaced magic with technology, putting your faith in things that you created with your own hands. The people here kept their faith in magic and saw no reason to press for advancements. Our lives are simple, by comparison, but it suits us."

"What magic?" Nikki asked.

The tavern owner smiled. "Magic that several of you possess or have encountered in your quests. Sorcery, wizardry, magical beasts... it all still exists here. But the oldest magic is our portals, and that's why you're here now."

"Portals?" Kevin asked.

The tavern owner nodded. "The world of Annwyn is comprised of two major continents and a number of very large islands. At first, only the continents were inhabited by humans. The rest were either uninhabited, or were the lands populated by magical beasts. People on one continent knew nothing of the people or the beasts on the other continents and islands. We had no way to easily travel and explore our world back then.

"But thousands of years ago—no one is sure exactly how long ago it was—Annwyn was visited by beings who possessed great magic and power. They appeared out of a thunderstorm and terrified the people who witnessed their arrival."

"That sounds like how we arrived here," Nikki commented.

"That's because it's *exactly* how you arrived here and how you were returned to your own world," the tavern owner confirmed. "Anyway, these beings, seeing how primitive the people here were, began teaching our ancestors many things. Then they built the portals. These portals connected the eight regions of our world that were most habitable by humans. The portals made it possible to travel to other parts of our world instantaneously. People were able to explore our world more easily, and colonies sprang up around the portals.

"These visiting beings selected one human to be the keeper of each portal, calling them Portal Keepers and giving them magical powers to control and protect each of the portals. These Portal Keepers are vitally important to us. After all, if you want to travel from one portal to another, but there are eight portals to choose from, you somehow have to be able to know which of the portals you are traveling to and from, right? That's what the Portal Keeper does. He or she opens the... corridor between portals so you can arrive at the correct destination."

The tavern owner took another drink from his tankard. "In time, our world was organized into the Eight Realms of Annwyn, or just the Eight Realms. One realm is for the High Kingdom, which rules the others, and the other seven are the kingdoms that rose from those early colonies. The Kingdom of Cockaigne, which you helped on your last quest, is one of the Eight Realms."

The tavern owner lowered his voice. "But there are more than eight portals on Annwyn. There are two others, which are not located within the borders of the Eight Realms. The first of these two is... here." The tavern owner gestured around the tavern. "The Portal of Riverstone is connected to your world. The visiting beings created this portal to bring more of your people here. Our environments were compatible, as were our people. We've brought people over a number of times over the eons. When your world experienced pestilence, war, natural disasters, plagues, depressions, we brought your people here for a new start and a chance to live. And when our own world experienced similar disasters, we brought people from your world to help us rebuild and repopulate. Our worlds truly are sister worlds, which is why this portal connects us. But since there is no working portal on your world, this portal cannot act like a doorway between, which is how the portals of the Eight Realms of Annwyn act. The forces of nature must be used to create a temporary portal to bring people here or send people there. That's why you experience lightning when you come here and return home. This portal has to create another portal in your world just long enough to move people back and forth."

Nikki and Justin looked at each other and nodded. "That makes sense," Nikki said. "But what about the last portal?"

"Ah, the Portal of Alesia," the tavern owner said. "That was the first portal that the visiting beings created. It is the master portal. It controls all other portals here. With it, you can create a new portal and link it to the others, you can shut down a portal, you can repair or move a portal, and you can search for new worlds to explore."

"New worlds?" Thor asked.

The tavern owner nodded. "The visiting beings had placed master portals on a number of worlds across the universe. The Portal of Alesia can connect to those portals, but it can also open temporary portals on new worlds that the Portal Keeper or his assistants might want to explore… to find a new home for our people, should there come a time when this world can no longer be inhabited. That portal connects us to the universe, just as the portals in the Eight Realms keep us connected to each other.

"By the way, you should know that the Portal of Cockaigne wasn't damaged when King Diarmaid's castle was destroyed, and its Portal Keeper is safe and healthy. I imagine King Rigderg will eventually want the portal moved closer to *his* castle, and that can be done quite easily using the Portal of Alesia."

"And what about these Portal Keepers?" Thor asked.

"Each Portal Keeper is chosen by his or her predecessor and by the portal itself. Portal Keepers do not answer to any king in any of the realms, including the High Kingdom. They serve their portal and nothing else. A

Portal Keeper cannot serve more than one portal. Once linked to a portal, the Keeper can never be linked to another one. Each Portal Keeper selects one or more assistants who help serve and protect the portal. Then, at the end of the Portal Keeper's life, a successor is chosen from the assistants to receive all of the Portal Keeper's knowledge and powers. The portal must agree with the choice, because the portal itself instructs the new Keeper how to use and maintain the portal."

"So the portal is... alive?" Thor asked.

"No... and yes," the tavern owner replied. "The portal has an intelligence that is beyond human understanding. If it's alive, it's not like any other life form you've ever encountered. But it is sentient. Of that, there is no doubt."

"So *you're* the Portal Keeper for the Portal of Riverstone," Allison stated. "You're the one who brings us here and sends us back home."

The tavern owner smiled and nodded. "I have been for a very long time. Portal Keepers' lives are much longer than those of most humans. The more powerful the portal, the longer the Portal Keeper lives. And our Grand Master, the Keeper of the Portal of Alesia, has lived the longest of us all. We answer to him and him alone, apart from our portals, and he answers to no man or woman. He commands us, and his portal commands the other portals. Whoever is the Grand Master is the most powerful person in our world... and that's the problem you're here to help me with."

"What do you mean?" Nikki demanded.

"The Grand Master, a man named Boreas, has disappeared, and all of his assistants were murdered. He's quite old. Ancient, in fact. And the time is growing near for him to choose his successor. Choosing a new Portal Keeper is a delicate process, but choosing the new Grand Master is even more so. I fear that someone has captured Boreas and is isolating him so he'll have choice but to make the kidnapper the new Grand Master. If that happens, if someone willing to kidnap and murder becomes the new Grand Master, there's no telling what he might do. He could blackmail the whole world by banishing people from Annwyn, isolating realms by shutting down their portals... all to increase his power and control over this world. It must not be allowed to happen."

"How long has the Grand Master been missing?" Justin asked.

"His disappearance was discovered shortly after you left us," the tavern owner replied. "Honestly, if you hadn't activated the game when you did, I would have been forced to break protocol and reach out to you for help. Of all the questers I've met over the years, there's no one else I trust to help with this problem more than the eight of you. I need you to find the Grand Master and return him to the Portal of Alesia before he has to select a successor. Barring that, you need to make certain that the kidnapper does not become the successor."

"What if the Grand Master dies without a successor?" Thor asked, fascinated with the magic involved in the portals and the Portal Keepers.

"Then no one will be able to use or control the Portal of Alesia ever again, and eventually, as the other portals get damaged or require maintenance that only the master portal can provide, all of the portals will fail. We will be isolated from the universe, from your world, and from ourselves. It'll be as it was before the visiting beings first came and built the portals."

"And the portal itself can't just choose another successor?" Thor pressed.

The tavern owner shook his head. "Each Portal Keeper must prepare his successor first. Yes, the portal teaches the successor how to use the portal, but the Portal Keeper must provide knowledge before the successor can be accepted by the portal. It's a two-step process, and you can't skip the first step and go straight to the second one."

"So how do we find the kidnapper and the Grand Master?" Justin asked.

The tavern owner sighed. "If his assistants hadn't been killed, I'd suggest asking them. Either way, the quest starts in Alesia.

"Alesia isn't part of any of the Eight Realms, and no one from the Eight Realms can know where it is. It has no governing authority, apart from the Grand Master. As a result, it's not the easiest place to travel. There are few roads, and most of the structures lie along one road that runs to and from the portal. While Alesia is sparsely populated, there *are* people living there. To the west of the portal, there are two villages and several farms and ranches. Immediately east of the portal is the residence of the Grand Master and his assistants. It's technically a castle, but not in the fortification sense like you saw in Cockaigne. Farther to the east are several buildings that look like farmhouses or barracks. These buildings were created by the visiting beings who made the portals, and even though they're the oldest structures on this world, they haven't aged a bit."

"How many buildings are there?" Justin asked.

"Ten or so," the tavern owner replied. "Personally, I

The Portal of Alesia

don't believe that anyone from Alesia is behind or involved in what has happened. They serve the Grand Master, and they'd gladly lay down their lives to protect him and the portal. No, whoever has done this must be an outsider, and that is one of the things that concerns me the most. No one is supposed to know exactly where Alesia is, so how did someone get there? That's what you'll need to discover. Fortunately, I have a way to get you there quickly. Then you'll need to use your various skills to find the kidnapper."

The tavern keeper looked at Thor with a strange expression on his face. "Thor, you might be able to get information from the portal itself."

"How?" Thor asked. "I'm not a Portal Keeper."

"No, but you're a sorcerer—a magical creature in this world. It might respond to your magic." Turning to Livvy, he added, "Or it may respond to yours, Livvy. You have nothing to lose by trying, and if it will share clues with you, it might make your quest easier to complete."

Nikki, Justin, and their teammates discussed the quest.

"It's nice to know that we're not trapped inside a game," Kevin said, "but it's a little strange to think that we're on a totally different world right now."

"I wonder how the game fits into all this," Peter said.

"It's how I find people to come here for quests," the tavern owner said as he brought over more food to the table. "The portal helped create the game, and by that I mean it provided the inspiration to the original game designer. Using the portal, I watch the players to identify people who could help us here."

"But why?" Nikki asked.

"Remember I told you that we prefer the simple life here? Well, there are side effects to that way of living. Curiosity and problem solving has become less prevalent in our cultural makeup. As a result, when there is a major problem to be solved, I get called upon to... import problem solvers from your world. Then I send you back before anyone knows where you came from. Oh, everyone knows that I hire the questers, but no one knows that you don't come from Annwyn. They simply assume that you're from one of the Eight Realms or from Riverstone itself, and I don't discourage that notion. It keeps the peace, so to speak."

"How do you plan to get us to Alesia?" Livvy asked.

"All of the Portal Keepers can travel between their portal and the Portal of Alesia when we meet with the Grand Master," the tavern owner explained. "I can send you through the portal here to Alesia. Apart from your world, it's the only other destination that the Portal of Riverstone can access."

Something occurred to Nikki. "Are our horses still here?" she asked.

"The horses that were gifts from the Duke and the new King you helped are here waiting for you. The horses you acquired from the late Viscount have been replaced with more reliable mounts. They're waiting in the stables."

Justin stared at the tavern owner. "Is there anything you can tell us about the kidnapper? What kind of power would he have to possess to do what he did?"

"You mean magic or other abilities like that?" the tavern owner asked.

Justin nodded.

The Portal of Alesia

"I don't know," the tavern owner admitted, worried. "It's reasonable to assume that he has some powers, but whether he's a wizard, a sorcerer, a shapeshifter, or some other magical or semi-magical being remains to be seen."

"You boosted our powers to deal with shapeshifters when we completed the last quest," Nikki noted. "Is that because we're going to face a shapeshifter in this quest?"

"I'm not sure, but it's possible." The tavern owner stroked his chin. "The portal suggested those upgrades to your powers and abilities, so it must have had a good reason."

"When do we head out?" Justin asked.

"At first light," the tavern owner replied. "I'll need to open the doors for the evening crowd soon, and the last thing I need is for one of them to see a portal open in my establishment. Knowing is one thing. Seeing is another."

The Quest Begins

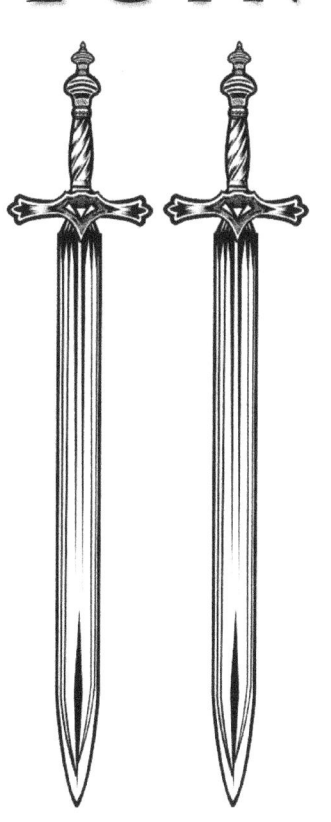

Chapter 2

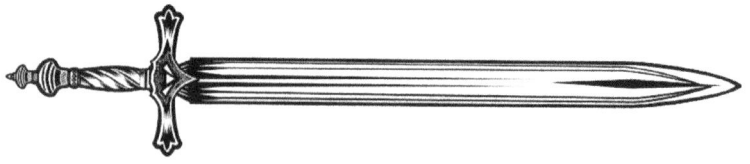

Before dawn the next morning, Livvy and Thor got up early—making certain not to wake Kevin and Bethany—got dressed, and went to find the tavern owner. There was a question they needed answered.

They met at the top of the stairs, looked at each other, and grinned.

"Let me guess," Thor whispered. "You want to know if you still have your powers when you shapeshift?"

Livvy's eyes opened wide, and she nodded. "It's only understandable. We have a new ability after our last quest. I think it might be better to know how it works *before* we find ourselves in a compromising situation."

"I agree," Thor said, gesturing for Livvy to go downstairs first. "I stayed awake all night thinking about it, wanting to test it and afraid to at the same time."

"Me, too."

The tavern owner was behind the bar when they got downstairs, but apart from him, the room was deserted.

The smell of baking bread filled the room, and sausages on iron skewers were cooking over the hearth of the fireplace. The aroma was intoxicating, and it made Thor and Livvy's stomachs rumble.

"Good morning, courageous questers. What brings the two of you down here so early?"

"We have a question regarding our ability to shapeshift," Thor responded.

The tavern owner just smiled. "I thought as much. What's your question?"

"Do our other powers and abilities still work when we're in another form?" Livvy asked.

"Yes."

"Even if we're in a non-human form?" Livvy pressed.

"Of course." The tavern owner gestured toward Livvy's heart. "Your powers and abilities are part of *you* when you're here. They're not tied to the form you've chosen to disguise yourself in. As long as you're you, your powers and abilities are with you."

Livvy looked relieved as she glanced at Thor. "Should we test shapeshifting before the others wake up?"

Thor nodded. The tavern owner explained how shapeshifting worked, and Livvy and Thor tried to follow his instructions.

It took several attempts for Thor to change his shape and then change back, but Livvy—who had the ability to change the shape of others—managed to change herself and change back much more quickly.

"Will shapeshifting drain our powers?" Livvy asked after she and Thor had successfully changed into another shape, used their powers, and then changed back. Livvy also forced Thor back into his real shape, which was one of their new powers.

"No," the tavern owner confirmed. "Shapeshifting is an ability, meaning it's a part of you. Your powers can get drained, but not your abilities. See the difference?"

Thor and Livvy nodded.

"Since you both have the ability detect a fellow shapeshifter and force him—or her—back into his original form, you should work with Nikki and Justin to practice this ability. They have it, too, and if they need to use it, they need to know what they're doing."

"We will," Thor promised.

Nikki, Justin, and the others came downstairs a while later. They saw Thor and Livvy with the tavern owner at the bar, and they walked over to the bar and joined them.

"What are you doing down here?" Kevin asked.

"Practicing one of our new abilities," Livvy answered, giving Kevin a good morning kiss.

"I never heard you get up," Bethany said, snuggling next to Thor.

"I didn't want to wake you," he said softly. "But this shapeshifting business had me curious, and I couldn't sleep. Evidently Livvy was having the same problem. But now we understand how it works, and we've learned that our powers still work no matter what form we take. We also learned how to force another shapeshifter back into their original form."

"We need to teach the two of you how to do this," Livvy said to Nikki and Justin. "You have this ability, too, and you'll need to know how to use it."

The tavern owner cleared his throat to get the questers' attention and handed over a bag of coins to Justin, who tied it to his sword belt.

"No map?" Nikki asked.

"Not this time. Where you're going isn't on any map you're allowed to see, and it's best that it remain that way. As I mentioned, Alesia isn't part of any of the Eight Realms, and no one from the Eight Realms can know where it is. Its only governing authority is the Grand Master." Looking at the questers, the tavern owner added, "Now you need to get your horses and your supplies. Once you've loaded up your horses, you'll need to lead them in here. I'll open the portal, and you'll have to lead your horses through. Horses get spooked enough going through a portal without having to deal with a rider."

Justin grabbed a lantern from the bar, and the questers exited the tavern and walked around the building to the stables. It was still dark outside, and the light streaming from the tavern's first-floor windows cast a yellowish glow on the ground. Wind rustled the leaves in the trees, but there were no other sounds.

When they reached the stables, Justin hung the lantern on the hook next to the entrance. Then he used a stick to light the other lanterns around the stables, the tack shed, and the supply shed.

Nikki recognized her horse immediately, and it seemed to recognize her. She stroked its head gently and slipped it an apple she had procured from the barrel outside the stables. The horse munched the apple as Nikki checked to make certain that the horse's fur was free of debris or anything that could irritate the horse's skin if trapped beneath the saddle or the straps.

The Portal of Alesia

Satisfied that the horse had been kept well-groomed, she retrieved the leather tack from the tack shed next to the stables. She let the horse smell the tack and then began saddling her horse. She started by placing the reins over the horse's head, putting the bit into the horse's mouth, setting the headpiece of the bridle over the horse's ears, and tightening the bands to keep the bridle in place. Then she placed a blanket on the horse's back and put the saddle on the blanket. She fastened and tightened the girth, and then she adjusted the stirrups to the proper length.

Once she was finished, Nikki led her horse to the supply shed and tied it to the hitching post next to Justin's mount. She joined Justin inside to gather and pack the supplies she'd need.

"It all looks exactly the same as last time," Nikki commented as she reached for a bow and three quivers of arrows.

"Except that I doubt Livvy will be turning Kevin into a cat this time," Justin said with a grin, pointing to the other cat they had seen the last time.

Nikki giggled. "I forgot about that. He certainly recovered from that incident, didn't he? Besides being turned into a cat, he has been a wolf once, a hawk once, and a dragon twice that I'm aware of."

"And he's completely in love with Livvy," Justin added with a whisper, "although I don't think they've used that word yet."

"Only the two of us have, as far as I know," Nikki said softly.

As they loaded up their supplies, Justin asked, "Hey, in all the excitement I forgot to ask how your appointment went with Dr. Alvarado on Friday."

"It was good," Nikki said, grabbing her filled saddlebags and placing them on her horse. "I told her about you and what you said to me that turned my thinking around. Obviously, I didn't tell her the context of that conversation, since she'd have me committed if I told her that I met you in a fantasy world where we were fighting for our lives against a wizard. But I did give her enough background that she was impressed with how you saw through my façade and told me exactly what I needed to hear to snap me out of my trust... delusions. She wanted me to congratulate you on getting through to me so quickly. I didn't bother to tell her the ways I've been showing you my gratitude."

Justin chuckled. "Probably for the best. I assume your trust issues are in the past?"

"As far as I know," Nikki answered. "You'll let me know if you see them resurface?"

"Always." Justin kissed her.

"Okay, you two," Kevin said as he tied his horse next to Nikki's. "Save that for when you're alone."

Nikki grinned at him. "And will you do the same with Livvy?"

Kevin blushed and said nothing.

The others led their horses to the supply shed, and there was no more time for conversation. They had to finish selecting and packing their supplies and then lead the horses inside the tavern before sunrise.

Once the supplies had been gathered and packed, and the lanterns had been blown out, the tavern owner and his

The Portal of Alesia

employees helped lead the horses into the tavern. The tables and benches had all been stacked around the edges of the room, leaving an open space in front of the bar for the horses and questers.

The wall next to the stairs leading up to the guestrooms was the only wall empty of tables and benches.

"That's where the portal will open," the tavern owner said.

The tavern owner and his employees closed and barred the doors and windows. "Is everyone ready?" the tavern owner asked the questers.

Nikki and Justin looked at their teammates and nodded.

"We're ready," Justin said.

"Very well. Hold tightly to your horses' reins," the tavern owner warned. He bowed his head in concentration. A moment later, a green glow appeared in the center of the empty wall. The glow took on an oval shape, and then the center of the oval parted, showing a green forest illuminated by dawn's first light. A large structure was visible halfway up the hill on the right.

"That's Alesia," the tavern owner said. "And that building is the Grand Master's home. I suggest making that your first stop."

He motioned for the questers to enter the portal. "Hurry up. I don't want to keep the portal open longer than necessary."

Justin went first, followed by Nikki.

Unlike the portal that brought the questers to Annwyn, there was no sensation as the questers passed from the tavern to Alesia. It was like walking through a doorway.

Once on the other side of the Portal, Nikki looked back at the others as they followed her through. The portal was at the base and in the center of an ancient tree. She could see a stone arch defining the boundaries of the portal, but vines, branches, and the tree itself had grown over the stones. Phosphorescent moss covered the top of the portal, giving off a soft glow.

Once all of the teammates were through the portal, the tavern owner waved at the questers, and then the portal closed. The green light of the portal faded, but the glowing moss continued to give off yellow and blue light.

Nikki rubbed her horse reassuringly and gave it another apple to eat. The others did the same.

Justin pointed to the Grand Master's residence. "I guess we should head there first."

"You go on without us," Thor said, motioning to Livvy. "We'll stay here and see if we can learn anything from the portal about what happened."

Justin nodded. "Don't be long."

As the others rode for the Grand Master's residence, Livvy said, "You're fascinated by these portals, aren't you?"

Thor nodded. "To think that this world was populated essentially from our world turns everything I know about history on its head. There have been mass, unexplained disappearances documented throughout time. Now I discover that many of those people were transported here through a portal. What other stories from antiquity can be attributed to visiting beings who came, taught, and left behind powerful objects that we've forgotten about? It's unsettling for a history professor to learn that historical events he thought would never be explained can actually be explained... but in a way no one will ever believe. Yes, I'm fascinated."

He motioned for Livvy to step forward toward the portal. "You're the one gifted with communicating. Why don't you try first?"

Livvy nodded and handed Thor her horse's reins.

She walked up to the portal, treading carefully around and over the moss and exposed roots that covered the ground. Once inside the stone archway, she touched the stones on either side. She concentrated, and then her head jerked up.

"What?" Thor asked, excited.

"Music," Livvy said. "I hear music. I think that's how the portal... communicates."

She tried harder, but all she could detect was the most beautiful music she had ever heard. She stepped further into the stone structure that framed the portal, and the music continued. Livvy walked all the way through to the other side, turned around, and walked back.

"All I can hear is the music," she said when she reached Thor. "I don't know if it's from this portal, or if all of the portals are creating the music together, but it's beautiful. You should try."

Thor handed her the reins of both horses and stepped forward. He placed his hands on the sides of the portal entrance. At first, he heard the music that Livvy heard, but then he began to see images in his mind. They moved slowly at first, but then they began to flash much faster. Without warning, images poured into his consciousness like the opening of a floodgate. He sank to his knees as he struggled to accept what the portal was showing him. And all the while, the music continued filling his mind.

Livvy stepped forward, but Thor motioned for her to

stay back.

And then the images stopped, and only the music remained. Thor looked around, realized he was kneeling on the ground, and stood up. He looked at Livvy.

"What happened?" she asked.

"I heard the music, but I also saw things. Many images. I still can't process all of it. It showed me... so much."

"Did it show you what happened to the Grand Master or his assistants?"

Thor nodded slowly. "I know it did, but I still don't know what the images meant or if they were in any particular order. I need time to... understand."

"Let's get up to the Grand Master's residence and tell the others," Livvy suggested.

Thor nodded, took the reins of his horse, and followed the road from the portal to the residence, where the rest of the team had gone.

The portal sat in the center of a valley between two ridges. The base of the valley looked like a dried-up riverbed that had disappeared in the far distant past. The Grand Master's residence was on the southern ridge, just over halfway up. The northern ridge was overgrown with trees and dense shrubs.

From the trees, halfway up the northern ridge across from the Grand Master's residence, four men watched Thor and Livvy head up the road away from the portal.

"The boss was right," the tall bearded man said quietly. "Someone *did* send a party to find out what

The Portal of Alesia

happened here. We need to get back and tell Atreus."

"And we need to tell Atreus that one of them communicated with the portal," the one-eyed blond man said. "He won't be pleased to find that out. No, he won't be pleased at all. He wants that portal for himself."

The one-eyed blond man turned to the other two men. "Go find Atreus and let him know what we saw." He gestured to the tall bearded man. "We'll keep any eye on these people—especially the one that the portal spoke to."

The two men slipped away from their hiding place and crept back to their horses. The tall bearded man and the one-eyed blonde man moved down the hill and quietly followed Thor and Livvy.

The Grand Master's residence was deserted. The tavern owner was right; it wasn't like the castles the questers had seen in Cockaigne, with walls, towers, and a central keep. This was more like a chateau made of stone and timbers. It was designed for comfort, rather than defense. Instead of arrow slits in the walls, leaded glass windows faced in all directions.

The questers searched every room on every level, but no one was there. A quick search of the grounds led to the grisly discovery of five bodies. They had been dead for some time—their bones nearly picked clean by carrion birds and other animals.

"These must be the Grand Master's assistants," Justin said. "The tavern owner said they had been murdered."

Bethany looked at the men closely. "It looks like they were all killed with sharp blades, either stabbed or their throats were cut. You can see the blade marks on their bones." Standing, she added, "We really shouldn't leave them like this."

"Hello? Where is everyone?" It was Thor's voice, coming from inside the residence.

"Out back," Justin shouted.

Thor and Livvy arrived a couple of minutes later. Livvy saw the bodies and shuddered.

"The Grand Master's assistants?" Thor asked.

Bethany nodded. "I was just saying that we shouldn't leave them this way."

"I'll take care of burying them," Thor offered.

"We'll put the horses in the stables," Justin said. "Then we can tell you what we found, and you can tell us what happened down at the portal."

Thor nodded. The other questers went back inside the residence. Thor used sorcery to dig graves, move the bodies into their individual resting places, and cover the bodies with dirt and turf. Then he followed the others into the residence.

There were no animals in the stables, but there was plenty of hay, feed, and water in each of the stalls. Once the horses settled in for the day, Justin and the others carried their supplies into the residence, which had its own spring water well in the kitchen.

"What did you find when you searched this place?" Livvy asked.

"The Grand Masters kept notes of every time the portal was used," Nikki said. "I found hundreds of journals in the library down the hall, and they were all filled with notations of when the portal was used, by whom, how many people came through... things like that. There were also journals on every new world the Grand Masters and their assistants explored, and the worlds they visited where portals already existed. It's fascinating information."

"What did you discover from the portal itself?" Justin asked.

Livvy described the music she heard from the portal. Thor described the music, and when he mentioned the images he saw, Justin asked, "Can you make sense of what you saw? Did the portal show you who took the Grand Master?"

"I'm not sure," Thor admitted. "I was a lot of images. I need to sort it out in my head before I can understand what it all meant."

"Maybe the journals in the library could help explain what you saw," Nikki suggested.

Thor nodded. "I'll check there first."

"In the meantime," Justin said, "Nikki, Kevin, Peter, and I will explore the area and see if we can find a trail left behind by the kidnapper. If we can find which way he took the Grand Master, we'll know where to start looking."

"Can Kevin stay here?" Livvy asked. "I think some aerial reconnaissance might be in order to find out what, and who, is around here, and since Kevin has been a bird before, I thought he might show me how to fly. Besides, two birds can cover more territory than just one."

Justin nodded. "That's a good idea. It might be a good idea to see if anyone is watching this place, and if so, you can read their minds and find out why and who sent them."

"You think we're being watched?" Livvy asked.

Justin shrugged. "I don't know. Something feels... off. It's like we're being watched, but I'm not sure. You're better with things like that than I am."

Livvy nodded. And like Justin, she felt uneasy for some reason. If they *were* being watched, she wanted to know who was doing it and why.

"What do you want Bethany, Allison, and me to do while you're gone?" Thor asked.

"Keep searching this place and see if those journals tell you anything useful," Justin said. "And try to figure out what the portal was trying to tell you."

Chapter 3

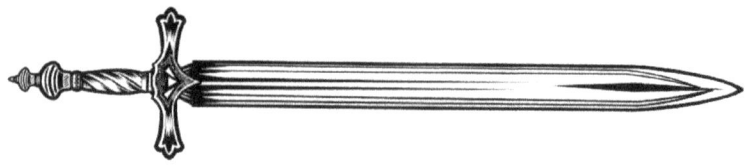

Livvy and Kevin climbed the stairs to the roof, where there was an unobstructed view of the surrounding region.

"What are you going to change us into?" Kevin asked.

"I was thinking hawks," Livvy replied. "I don't want to pick a bird that could be considered prey to some random predator."

"Interesting..." Kevin smirked.

"What's interesting?"

"You know that hawks mate for life, right?"

"Look, Kevin, if you're suggesting we try some kinky bird sex, the answer is no. I prefer the human kind."

Kevin laughed. "I wasn't suggesting anything of the sort. It was just an observation."

Livvy looked at him, and then she got a mischievous twinkle in her eye. "You know wolves mate for life, too, don't you?"

Kevin nodded. "And you turned me into one of those

on our last quest. We could both be wolves together on this quest, but that would just prove my point."

"Which is?"

"That we keep turning into things that mate for life. Is that your subtle way of telling me something?"

"Like what?" Livvy asked innocently.

Kevin looked deeply into her eyes, and Livvy felt her knees weaken and butterflies in her stomach. "That you see us as mated for life," Kevin said.

"But what about dragons?" Livvy asked to keep from answering the question. "I've never heard that they mate for life."

"And I don't want to go up to one and ask it, so let's assume they do and leave it at that," Kevin replied. "And you didn't respond to my statement. Do you see us as mated for life?"

"We really should get going," Livvy said, glancing up at the sunlight filling the valley below them.

"Not until you answer me."

"Is this really the time for this?"

Kevin said nothing. He just held her gaze.

Livvy stamped her foot. "Okay, fine. Yes, I see us mated for life. Satisfied?"

Kevin stepped forward and took Livvy in his arms. "Deliciously. That wasn't so hard, was it? I've known I wanted to be mated to you for life for a while. Now that you've finally admitted it, I think we have some planning to do. In fact, I have an idea or two I'd like to run past you."

"Another time, lover boy." Livvy gave him a quick kiss. "We have work to do."

Kevin winked at her. "Okay. You're right. We're burning daylight. Transform us both, and I'll teach you how to fly."

Livvy concentrated. A moment later, she was looking at the most beautiful hawk she had ever seen before. Then she looked at herself. Seeing feathers covering her body, feeling her talons gripping the roof tiles, and hearing the hawk's cry instead of her own voice was a new experience, but it felt exhilarating.

Through their mental connection, Kevin explained to her how to fly, and she practiced flying around the roof a couple of times. Then she felt ready to explore the region with Kevin.

They flew over Nikki, Justin, and Peter, who were leading their horses as they looked for the kidnapper's trail. Livvy and Kevin cried out, circled them once, and then flew off to survey the territory and look for anyone watching the Grand Master's residence.

Nikki looked up when she heard two hawks crying. She waved, and they flew off to start searching the region around the Grand Master's residence.

"That was Livvy and Kevin," Nikki said.

"I thought it might be," Justin replied.

"Where should we start looking?" Peter asked.

Justin pointed down toward the portal. "I didn't see anything as we rode up to the residence." Then he pointed up toward the top of the ridge. The road from the portal to the Grand Master's residence continued toward the top of the ridge, and there was dense foliage surrounding the residence. "I suggest looking up that way. If they used horses to take the Grand Master away, they'd need a road, or at least a wide path. Since this appears to be the only road around, we should check it out first. If we don't find anything, we can search the road from the residence down to the portal to see if they went through the valley between the two ridges or if they crossed over to the northern ridge. But I don't want to split up until we're certain there's no one watching us. I don't want one of us cut off."

Nikki and Peter nodded and led their horses after Justin toward the top of the ridge.

The three of them were expert trackers, and they searched the ground and the branches on both sides of the road for any signs of someone riding or walking recently.

There were signs all along the road, both of horses and men walking toward and away from the Grand Master's residence. Whoever had passed this way didn't bother to hide their tracks.

When they reached the top of the ridge, Nikki saw the two hawks in the distance, flying in wide circles. As she looked around, she was awed by the natural beauty all around her. "What a sight," she whispered.

"I agree," Peter said. "It's so... unspoiled. Pristine. Not too many places left on Earth like this."

Justin nodded in agreement as he took in the sights. Then he looked at the trail they had been following. "The tracks continue along this road," he said.

"I want to keep following the trail," Nikki said. "But, I'm curious about that ridge over there." She pointed to the ridge opposite where they were standing. "Something keeps telling me we need to check over there, too. Plus, I don't want to get too far from the residence until we hear back from Livvy and Kevin. There could be a whole army of people camped a mile from here, and we'd never know it. I don't want to ride into something we can't handle."

Justin looked up at the sun. It was approaching mid-morning, and the sky was clear. "Okay, this trail isn't going anywhere, as long as it doesn't rain. Let's explore the opposite ridge, and then we'll go back to the residence and wait to hear from our hawk friends. Who knows? Maybe Thor will have something to tell us by then."

They mounted their horses and rode down the hill toward the Grand Master's residence and the portal beyond.

While Bethany and Allison searched the residence again, Thor headed for the library. As a history teacher, he had spent much of his career in libraries, researching tedious details, hoping to find the data that either proved his premise or led him to the answer he was looking for.

He started reading the journals, analyzing the notes about every time the Portal of Alesia had been used to explore Annwyn, to create or repair the other portals, to explore the worlds that had master portals on them, and to explore new worlds.

After an hour, he found the information fascinating, but he also discovered that he was exhausted from lack of sleep the night before. He could barely keep his eyes open. He decided to close his eyes for a few minutes.

Sleep took him quickly.

As he slept, Thor began dreaming. The images shared by the portal arranged themselves into a chronological sequence, and in his dream, Thor saw everything that had happened with the Grand Master and his assistants over the previous several weeks.

The first thing Thor saw was the portal opening and thirty or forty men coming through with their horses late at night. They mounted as soon as they were through the portal and rode up the valley until the valley and the main road intersected a few miles east of the Grand Master's residence. There were no lights in the residence. The men had arrived unobserved, and they rode to a large building a few hours away. The building looked like the cross between a farmhouse and a country mansion. It was a large stone structure, and it appeared to be deserted. Thor saw several similar-looking buildings in the distance, and in his dream, he knew that these were the buildings made by the beings who created the portals.

The next thing Thor saw was men watching the Grand Master and his assistants. He saw them spy on the Grand Master as he trained his assistants to one day succeed him. He saw the spies report what they had learned to the kidnapper, whose face was blurred.

Thor saw the kidnapper take on the appearance of the Grand Master. He approached the assistants, distracting them from seeing his men until it was too late. The assistants were soon dead. The kidnapper then changed his appearance to that of one of the assistants. He called out for the Grand Master, who appeared a moment later. His men captured the Grand Master, and when the kidnapper changed back to his true form, the Grand Master saw his assistants dead on the ground.

"What's the meaning of this?" he demanded.

"You and your portal are going to choose a new successor," the kidnapper said. "Me."

With that, the kidnapper led the spies and the Grand

Master to the waiting horses. They rode up the ridge and disappeared from sight.

Thor saw the kidnapper and the Grand Master approaching the building that the kidnapper and his men rode to when they first arrived.

The Grand Master was taken to a room halfway down a long corridor, and he was locked inside.

"Don't bother trying to escape, Boreas," the kidnapper said contemptuously. "There's no escape for you but death."

Thor woke up with a start. He had no idea how long he had been asleep, but he now understood everything that the portal had tried to tell him. He looked up and saw Bethany and Allison watching him.

"A shapeshifter," Thor said. "The kidnapper is a shapeshifter."

Livvy and Kevin flew west of the portal and saw where the villages, farms, and ranches were located. They found a road that went from the villages, around the portal, and up the ridge where Nikki, Justin, and Peter were searching.

Next, they flew east, over the Grand Master's residence, and toward the stone structures that the tavern owner indicated were built by the visiting beings eons ago.

"There are people inside those buildings," She said to Kevin as they flew over the first two stone structures. *"I can sense them."*

"How many can you sense?" Kevin asked.

"Thirty at least. Maybe forty altogether. But there are two who are different from the others. One who is

extremely old, and one who is filled with rage and fear."

"The old one is probably the Grand Master," Kevin noted. "I wonder if the other one is the kidnapper. Do you want to get closer to those two buildings, or do you want to search the other buildings?"

Livvy looked east, where the rest of the stone structures were. "It'll take quite a while to search them all, and besides, I'm starting to get the urge to hunt."

"That's normal," Kevin told her. "The longer you're in a particular shape, the more of its instincts start trying to control your actions."

"Then let's head back. I still want to see if anyone is watching the Grand Master's residence."

"Okay."

They flew west and saw Nikki, Justin, and Peter searching the northern ridge opposite the Grand Master's residence. She circled them a couple of times, and then she and Kevin flew toward the residence.

As they circled the building, Livvy saw two men watching the Grand Master's residence from the dense brush next to the road.

"Two men watching the castle," she said to Kevin. "They're hidden along the road leading to the portal."

She reached out with her mind and read their thoughts. It didn't take long to learn all about them and the man they worked for—a man named Atreus, who had orchestrated the kidnapping of the Grand Master.

"We need to get back to the residence and tell the others," Livvy said. "I know who the kidnapper is and where he's holding the Grand Master."

"Do you know how to get there?" Kevin asked.

"Yes. He's in the second of those two stone buildings

we saw east of here. I saw the landmarks they use to get there. We should be able to use those to find the place."

As Livvy and Kevin headed back to the Grand Master's residence, they saw Nikki, Justin, and Peter coming up the road. After making certain that the watchers wouldn't see them change shape, Livvy led Kevin toward the road and transformed back into their human forms.

"How was flying, Livvy?" Nikki asked after she got over the surprise of seeing two hawks land in front of them.

"It was great, and we have a lot to tell you," Livvy replied. "We should go inside. There are prying ears a little way down the road from here, and we don't want them hearing what I discovered when I read their minds."

"Thor? Bethany? Allison? Where are you?" Nikki called out when she and the others entered the residence.

"In the library," Bethany called back.

"We'll be right there. And we have news."

"So does Thor."

Once everyone was seated in the library, Justin asked, "So, who wants to go first?"

Livvy raised her hand. "There are two men watching this place. They're hiding just down the road between here and the portal. They work for a man named Atreus, who is the kidnapper. He instructed four men to keep an eye on the portal in case anyone came through it. When we arrived, two rode back to tell Atreus. The ones I saw stayed here to see what we're up to."

"We must have ridden right past them when we checked out the ridge opposite this one," Nikki said. "There were signs that four men had been watching the residence from over there, but we couldn't tell when they abandoned that position."

Livvy looked at Thor. "They're particularly interested in you, Thor, because the portal spoke to you."

"I imagine they wouldn't be happy if they knew what the portal said to me," Thor commented.

Livvy's eyes went wide. "You understand the images?"

Thor nodded. "I was reading the journals, and I got sleepy. I closed my eyes, and I started dreaming. The images from the portal started making sense, and I saw everything that happened here. Atreus is a shapeshifter. His henchmen killed the Grand Master's assistants, and then they captured the Grand Master. They dragged him onto a horse, and they rode up the ridge and to the east. I saw where they took him. It's a large stone building, sort of a cross between a farmhouse and one of those country mansions you see in France. It was one of the buildings the tavern owner told us about. The Grand Master was still alive as of a week ago."

"The kidnapper is a shapeshifter? That explains a lot," Justin said. "Why was the Grand Master kidnapped?"

"This Atreus wants to be the next Grand Master, and he wants the old Grand Master to make certain that happens. That's why all the assistants were murdered."

"We saw a number of large stone buildings east of here," Livvy said. "We didn't see any armies or anything like that, but at least two of those buildings are inhabited by thirty or forty men total. When I read the minds of the two guys watching this place, I saw the landmarks they use to ride back to Atreus' headquarters. I don't know if that's where they're holding the Grand Master, but it should help us find him."

"We found the trail they took when they left here," Justin said. "We should be able to follow it, and between what Thor saw, and what you saw and learned from those two watchers, we should be able to find where they're holding the Grand Master and free him."

"Do you want to get started after we eat something?" Nikki asked.

Justin shrugged. "Livvy, how far away were these buildings you saw?"

"The closest ones were three... maybe four hours east of here. Wouldn't you agree, Kevin?"

Kevin nodded. "Definitely several hours east of here, unless we galloped most of the way. It would be nearly dark by the time we got there, and we could miss the landmarks that Livvy identified, or it could be too dark for Thor to determine which building is the right one. And don't forget, there are several similar buildings spread out in the distance farther east. If we have to search all of them, it'll take time. I'd rather not try a rescue and escape in darkness, nor do I want to make camp where we could be seen. It might be best to get an early start tomorrow. Livvy and I could make a more detailed reconnaissance of the area, meet the rest of you on the road, and then we could make a plan while *en route*."

Justin looked at Thor. "What do you think, Thor? If the portal showed you what happened and where they took the Grand Master, did you see anything else that might help us?"

Thor leaned back in his chair. "Only that thirty or forty men came though the portal in the dead of night and headed toward those stone structures east of here. As much as I'd like to get started now, waiting until morning might be best. I suggest we eat and then turn in for the night. If we can be ready to go a few hours before dawn, then we could reach those buildings a couple of hours after sunrise, and we could get away from here before the men watching us know we've gone."

Justin looked around the room. Nikki and Peter were nodding, as were Livvy and Kevin. "Bethany? Allison? Are you agreement?"

They nodded.

"Then that's the plan. Is there food in the kitchen, or do we need to dip into our rations?"

"There's plenty of food in the kitchen," Allison confirmed. "With Livvy's help, we should be able to have a fine meal before we retire for the night."

Dinner was excellent, and once the dishes were cleaned and put away, the couples retired to the four guest chambers that Bethany and Allison found on the third level of the residence.

Nikki entered the chamber she was sharing with Justin first, and he followed, locking the door behind him. Nikki turned and smiled.

"Just like old times," she said playfully.

"Old times?" Justin asked, putting down the pitcher of water, basin, and towels on the night table before walking over to her.

"Having to take off our armor before bed. We slept fully dressed last night."

Justin grinned. "I've gotten used to undressing you out

of your modern clothing. Not that I mind the extra work. It makes the anticipation more... exciting."

"If that's the case, I have armor at home, you know. We could try a little role play and see if it's as exciting there as it is here."

Justin chuckled. "We'll add that the list of things to try. But for now, I just want to get out of these clothes and into bed with you."

Nikki wrapped her arms around Justin's neck. "Then we shouldn't waste a second," she cooed as she leaned in for a kiss. In spite of the number of times they had made love, both on this world and back home, she felt that familiar warmth radiating from her core, spreading out until her fingertips tingled, longing for his skin to be touching hers.

The chamber was warm, so they decided to skip making a fire that night. They helped each other remove their armor and clothes, and soon they were standing naked in the low afternoon sunlight diffused through the dense trees outside.

"That's a sight I'll never tire of seeing," Justin said, taking Nikki into his arms. "You have the most perfect body I've ever seen, but there's so much more to you than physical perfection. You're everything I've ever wanted... could ever want. I don't want to live a day without you in it. Being without you is just no good for me anymore."

He began nuzzling her neck below her earlobes, kissing her gently as he held her.

Nikki's nipples were erect as her breasts pressed against his chest. She could feel wetness between her legs, and she longed to feel him inside of her. But she liked to give as well as receive pleasure, and this man that she loved was going to receive as much pleasure as she could give that night.

"I love you, Justin," she whispered. "You brought me back to life, and you make me feel alive every day. You brought the light back into my world, and I'll never be whole without you."

"I love you, Nichole." Justin had started using her full name when they were being intimate, after they had found each other back home. In his mind, it was their private name... one reserved just for him when they were about to become one.

Nikki grabbed the back of his head with both hands and brought it down so she could kiss him. The warmth she felt inside of her exploded as she felt his erection begin growing.

She pushed him toward the bed. He sat on the edge, and she rolled him to the center so he was on his back. Then she straddled him, with her head facing away from his. Before he knew it, his erection was in her mouth. He reached up, clutched her butt, and began licking her clit. She gasped as he found her sensitive spot, and then she began working her magic on him, both sucking tightly and licking him at the same time. Her head moved up and down, stimulating him until he had reached his full size.

She wanted him inside of her, but she also didn't want to stop pleasuring him. His breathing was in gasps as he approached the climax, and she decided to finish him in that position. She tightened her lips around him and began moving up and down faster.

Justin shuddered from the sensations. He tried to keep his tongue pleasuring her, but his breathing was so fitful that he had to switch to using his fingers to stimulate

The Portal of Alesia

her as his head sank back into the pillow. His fingers passed over her clit from left to right in a rapid motion, using her wetness as lubrication, stimulating her more strongly than she was used to.

The first orgasm hit her, and both of her legs were trembling from what Justin was doing. He increased the speed of his fingers, prolonging the orgasm and the quivering, which she could no longer control. She fought the urge to bite down, knowing that would cause him pain, but it was hard to maintain her lips' grip on him.

Finally, when she was worried that she'd have to break the connection, he climaxed, and she felt the hot, sticky liquid shooting into her mouth. She swallowed all of it and finally released him.

He flipped her over onto the far side of the bed and lay next to her while he continued stimulating her with his fingers. The next orgasm was so intense that she squirted, spraying the bed between her legs. She cried out as it happened, having never experienced anything like that before.

"What did you do to me?" she moaned, trying to catch her breath.

"That was just the beginning," he whispered.

He moved on top of her and penetrated deeply, still fully erect. As he thrust, she felt another orgasm hit, along with more squirting, which Justin seemed to enjoy. He climaxed inside of her, and when she felt his warmth shooting deep inside of her, she orgasmed again.

He rolled her onto her hands and knees and penetrated her again, keeping her on the far side of the bed. He gripped her hips in his hands and moved her forward and backward. Her legs began quivering again as the next orgasm hit, but his powerful hands kept her from falling flat on the bed. He kept her moving forward and backward until he climaxed. His cum was running down her inner thighs, but he wasn't done.

He rolled her over and began stimulating her with his fingers again.

"No," she whispered breathlessly. "I can't take it. I can't..."

The orgasm hit her, and she squirted. Her own fluids mixed with his as it shot out of her. At this point, her entire body was quivering uncontrollably, with her arms and legs in the air, shaking and trembling. Her stomach muscles spasmed again and again and again.

Justin slowly stopped what he was doing to her and gave her the chance to catch her breath. His cum was still running out of her, and the bedsheets were soaked on the far side of the bed. But the sheets on the other half of the bed were dry.

Justin grabbed two towels, wet one with the water in the pitcher, and began washing Nikki. Then he dried her with the second towel. After he washed himself, he pulled her over to the dry side of the bed and held her close.

"What did you do to me?" Nikki demanded, still panting. "I've never experienced anything like that before."

"Did you enjoy it?" Justin whispered.

"Well... yes, but it freaked me out. Is that normal?"

"I've heard that not every woman can experience an ejaculation. I wanted to see if you could. You can."

"So *that's* what that was. I've heard about it, but... wow. It was the most intense thing I've ever felt. Why does it have to be so messy?"

"Good question. Women don't know how to do

anything the easy way, do they?"

Nikki playfully popped him in the shoulder. "You're a wicked man, Justin Bradford, but I love you anyway."

"And I love you, Nichole Frasier. Never doubt that."

The two men watching the Grand Master's residence were alerted by the sound of horses approaching. A moment later, the two men they sent to Atreus returned.

"What did Atreus say when you told him about the strangers?" the one-eyed blond man asked.

"He was pissed, as you guessed. He said to keep that guy away from the portal and away from him."

"Did he give any suggestions about how he wants us to do that?" the one-eyed blond man asked.

"Naw, just that he didn't want the guy to go near the portal or near him. Oh, he did say not to kill him, but nothing else."

The one-eyed blond man rubbed the back of his head. "I guess we could grab him and take him to the same place we took the old man. It's a big building with lots of rooms. That'll keep him away from the portal and away from Atreus, since he and the others are staying in a different location."

"Sounds like a good plan," the tall bearded man said.

The others agreed.

"Let's go get him."

CHAPTER 4

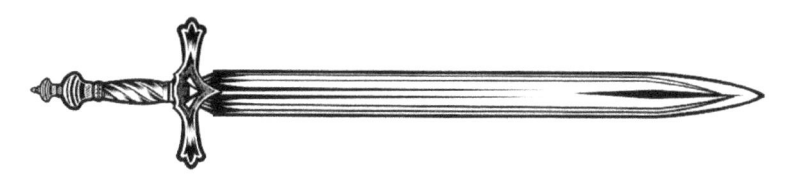

Boreas, Grand Master of the Portal Keepers and Keeper of the Portal of Alesia, sat in the empty room being used as his cell. He knew he was in one of the buildings that the beings who made the portals had constructed; he had explored them before when he was younger. He just didn't know which building he was inside.

He also knew that there was only one other person in the building with him—Atreus, his kidnapper.

Boreas knew why Atreus was the only other person near him. *He wants to be the next Grand Master. He thinks that the power will pass to him by default if he's the only human in my presence when it's my time to die. Oh, how little he knows of the power of the portals. It has already rejected him, and nothing he does will force the portal to accept him as the next Keeper. He might as well kill me now and get it over with. Keeping me alive won't serve his ends at all.*

But that wasn't the only thing Boreas was thinking

about. Something else troubled his mind.

He was still in communication with the portal, and he had learned something very interesting. *The portal spoke to someone. Not just with music, which magical beings can hear. No, the portal actually showed him images of what happened to my assistants and me. That's unusual... unusual indeed. Portals speak to the Keepers and their successors, not to the untrained and unprepared. This person must have great magical powers, but even then, no portal has spoken to someone untrained in being a Portal Keeper.*

But then again, no sorcerer has ever tried to communicate with a portal, to my knowledge.

Boreas had already figured out that it had to be a sorcerer who communicated with his portal. No one else could have that kind of power, except for the beings who originally built the portals.

Boreas heard someone approaching his cell. A moment later, the door opened, and Atreus, his kidnapper, appeared.

"Have you changed your mind, Boreas?" Atreus asked, contemptuously.

"You know that will never happen, shapeshifter," Boreas spat. "Besides. My portal will never accept you, so what does it matter if I change my mind? I've been telling you this ever since you brought me here. Nothing has changed. The portal wouldn't accept you then, and it won't accept you now. Why can't you understand that? Why do you insist on believing that it's my choice alone whether or not you become the next Grand Master?"

"Do you really think I won't kill you if you refuse me?" Atreus growled, ignoring everything that Boreas had said.

"Whether my death is at your hands or from old age makes no difference to me or to the portal. If I die without a successor that the portal accepts, then my portal will die, and in time, all other portals on Annwyn will die. You won't get the prize you seek as long as the portal has to accept my successor, and it will Never. Accept. You."

Boreas turned away and made a dismissive gesture toward Atreus. "Do what you wish with me, but stop asking me to name you as my successor. I cannot. I will not. So go away, and let me die."

Atreus' face grew evil. "Death won't come for you quickly or easily, old man. Count on that. I'll come back tomorrow, and you'd better have a different answer for me by then."

Atreus exited the room and slammed the door behind him. Boreas heard the lock turn.

Egotistical fool, he thought. *He simply cannot or will not accept that this is not my choice alone. The portal has to accept him. It won't, and neither will the other Portal Keepers.*

Boreas looked around the room, knowing that there was no way out. *I have a responsibility to my portal, to the other Portal Keepers, and to Annwyn to choose a successor that the portal will accept. Otherwise, I have failed in my duty to the visiting beings who first built the portals, and I have failed in my duty to this world. There must be a way to choose a successor before I die—one who is worthy and acceptable to my portal—but if there is, I certainly don't yet know what it is.*

The Portal of Alesia

Thor knew that the other three couples were either having sex or had already had sex up in their chambers, but he and Bethany were still in the library. Thor needed to review some of the portal journals again, and Bethany had decided to keep him company.

Thor knew that Bethany wanted to be making love to him upstairs, but her understanding of his nature kept her from saying anything. *Sometimes I think she deserves better,* Thor thought to himself as he watched her in the candlelight. *Being in a relationship with a research professor isn't easy... but then again, being in a relationship with a surgical nurse isn't easy either. I know we can find a happy balance, but this relationship is too new to have everything worked out. I should send her up to bed, but then again, I welcome the company.*

He closed the journal he had been studying and reached for the next one. "I'm sorry about this, Bethany," he said softly. "I know you'd rather be in bed, and I appreciate your company. I need to find something before I turn in... something that I remember from my dream earlier. I promise that once I find it, we can go upstairs."

Bethany flashed him a sleepy smile. "It's okay, Thor. I know this is important to the quest, so I don't mind waiting up with you. I just want to be with you, whether it's upstairs or here."

Thor stood and walked over to Bethany, who was sitting in an overstuffed wingback chair closer to the fireplace. "That means the world to me." He kissed her on the lips and then started giving her a shoulder massage, which she loved.

After a few minutes, she reached up and patted his hands, letting him know that he could stop. He kissed her forehead and turned to go back to the desk covered with the journals.

Darkness took him before he could take a step.

Before Bethany could scream, the one-eyed blond man put his hand over her mouth.

"Take the sorcerer outside to the horses," he ordered the other men. "I'll tie her up and be there in a minute."

The three other men, led by the tall bearded man, put a bag over Thor's head and dragged the unconscious man out of the library.

The one-eyed blond man bent down and said, "Listen closely, missy. I'm leaving you alive, because I have no orders to kill anyone. That goes for your friends upstairs. But if you follow us or try to rescue your lover boy, I will kill you all. Understand?"

Bethany nodded.

"Good. Now I'm going to tie you up and gag you. If you make a sound, I'll slit your throat and toss you in the fireplace there. Okay?"

Bethany, eyes wide with fear, nodded again.

The one-eyed blonde man pulled out a length of rope and tied Bethany's hands and feet together. Then he tied her to the chair so she couldn't get up. Next, he wadded up a piece of cloth. "Open wide," he commanded.

Bethany opened her mouth, and he shoved the cloth into it.

"Remember what I told you, missy," the one-eyed blond man said as he exited the library.

Bethany tried to free herself, but the man had tied her expertly. She was not getting loose without help.

She leaned back in the chair, terrified for Thor.

The one-eyed blond man joined the others outside. Thor had been thrown over the back of a horse, and his arms and legs had been tied together to keep him from falling off. The other men were already mounted and ready to go.

The one-eyed blond man vaulted into his saddle and motioned for the others to follow. They rode east up the ridge and disappeared into the night.

Even though the men had ridden to the ancient buildings many times, finding the way in the moonlight took longer than they anticipated. They arrived at the closest building just before sunrise, and then they turned and headed for the second building, where the old man was being kept.

As they approached the second building, they saw Atreus leave and head for the two buildings that were a couple of hours to the southeast.

"See?" the one-eyed blond man said. "Atreus isn't staying here, so this is the perfect place to dump the prisoner. It'll keep him away from Atreus, and it'll certainly keep him away from the portal."

They dismounted in front of the main entrance to the second building. One of the men cut Thor loose, and the others grabbed him and dragged him into the building. Halfway down the corridor, they stopped, opened the door of one of the rooms, and threw Thor inside. Then they placed some food and water inside the room, locked the door, exited the building, and rode back to the first building, which was being used as the barracks where most of Atreus' men were housed.

Thor had been conscious for several hours, and even though he could have freed himself and escaped at any time, he wanted to find out where he was being taken and why.

"If they hurt Bethany or the others, I'll incinerate them as painfully as possible," he vowed to himself as he was bounced along the road leading east.

When he was thrown into his cell, and the door was locked, he pulled the bag off his head and looked around. He was immediately impressed with the construction—the perfect angles, the smoothness of the stones, the way the stones fit together with no mortar or other cement that he could see. It was surprisingly exact engineering and not something he expected to find on this world.

"The visiting beings who built this place were splendid engineers," he thought.

He knew he could get out of the room easily. Exact engineering or not, he was a sorcerer and a shapeshifter. He had powers and abilities that would set him free in seconds. But before he went barging into a corridor that could be filled with guards, he decided to take a more cautious approach.

"Is anyone out there?" he shouted. "Can anyone hear me?"

Nothing.

He repeated himself.

This time, he heard someone reply, "Who are you?"

"Just a prisoner. Who are you?"

"An old man who's a prisoner, too," came the reply.

"How long have you been here?" Thor asked.

The Portal of Alesia

"A week... I think."

Thor had a strong feeling he knew who he was talking to. "Are you Boreas?"

"Where did you hear that name?" the voice demanded weakly.

"The portal told me in a dream," Thor replied.

"You... you're the sorcerer the portal told me about?"

"Yes," Thor replied.

"We need to talk," the voice said. "But not this way. Can you leave your cell?"

"Yes. Are there any guards around?"

"No. Only my kidnapper, Atreus, but I think he's somewhere else at the moment."

Thor placed his hand on the door, near the locking mechanism. A moment later, he heard the lock disengage. The door swung open, and Thor stepped into the corridor. He grabbed the food and water left for him, closed the door, and locked it again.

"Where are you?" Thor asked.

"Follow my voice," the voice replied.

The voice was coming from directly across the corridor. Thor unlocked the door and stepped inside.

Boreas was on the floor in front of him, looking very weak. Thor closed and locked the door behind him, and then he knelt next to the old man.

"My name is Thor," the sorcerer said.

Boreas' eyes lit up. "After the Norse god of thunder and war."

"You know Norse mythology?" Thor asked, surprised.

Boreas smiled. "I should. I lived in Oslo before I came here to Annwyn."

"I was there three years ago," Thor said. "It was just a

quick trip. I flew in for a long weekend and then flew home four days later. It wasn't enough time, but maybe I'll be able to go again..."

Thor noticed a puzzled look on Boreas' face. "You... *flew* there?"

Thor nodded. "Yes. I caught a plane to New York, and then changed planes for the flight to Oslo."

"You... caught a... plane?"

Thor finally understood. "When did you leave Oslo?"

"In the year of our lord seventeen-thirty-two. Why?"

"That was almost three hundred years ago, sir. It's now two-thousand-twenty-four."

"Really? How remarkable," Boreas said. "Am I really that old? I guess it's true that Portal Keepers live longer than most."

"Indeed," Thor agreed.

"And you can... *fly*?"

Thor smiled. "A lot has changed since you left Earth, sir. Man has built machines that can travel through the air. In your day, to travel from Oslo to New York would take weeks by sailing ship. It took less than seven hours to fly there from New York."

"Seven *hours*? That's incredible magic."

"No magic, just ingenuity," Thor said. "We no longer use horses or wagons for transportation. We have a machine that can travel so fast, that what used to take a day by horse now takes only an hour. We also have machines called trains that can cross entire continents in days. There's a train that goes from London to Paris... underneath the English Channel."

Boreas shook his head. "It staggers the imagination. I'd love to know more, but we have more pressing matters

The Portal of Alesia

to discuss. If the portal spoke to you, then it must trust you and accept you. It's rare for a portal to choose someone who hasn't been given proper instruction by a Portal Keeper first, but the situation being what it is... I guess things cannot proceed along their normal course."

"I need to get you out of here and back to your portal," Thor said. "We can't stay here."

"It's too late for that, my friend," Boreas said. "I'd never survive the trip, and even if I did, I have no assistants there to appoint as my successor."

"But don't you have to choose your successor before you die?" Thor asked. "And if you don't, won't your portal... die?"

Boreas nodded. "And the successor I choose must be accepted by my portal, too." Looking directly into Thor's eyes, he added, "But it seems that my Portal has already accepted someone. So all that remains is for me to name him my successor and provide what training I can in the time I have left."

Thor was confused by what Boreas had said, but then he heard the music from the portal in his mind again. His eyes opened wide. "Wait a minute. You mean *me*?"

"Yes," Boreas confirmed. "I need a successor that the portal will accept, and it would never have communicated with you if it didn't accept you. Your dream is proof of that."

"But I'm not from Annwyn, I'm from Earth. I have a life there. How can I leave all that behind and remain here as your successor?"

"How can you not?" Boreas asked. "You have been chosen... by a magic as old as time itself. This is your destiny, Thor. Of course, you can refuse, but if you do, you condemn this world to isolation and chaos. What do you think will happen when the portals of the Eight Realms begin to fail? Kingdom will make war on kingdom as each begins to strive for power, and who will win these wars? Not the people, I can assure you. It is the portals that have kept the realms at peace for hundreds and hundreds of years. Take away the portals, and all that makes Annwyn a peaceful world will collapse. Do we mean so little to you that you'd allow that to happen?"

Thor glared at the old man. "That's not fair. If I were of this world, I wouldn't hesitate to step in. But I'm not from here."

"Neither am I," Boreas reminded him, "and yet here we are. Both born on one world, and both called to safeguard another world. Destiny has called us both across the universe. Would you be here, now, if you weren't supposed to be here?"

"That's a philosophical question, sir. I'm a historian. I search the past for truth and fact. I don't pretend to interpret the meaning of the universe."

Boreas' shoulders slumped. "All right. You don't have to give me an answer now. Just think about it. But know this: The Portal of Alesia has never chosen wrong. It is incapable of choosing wrong. If it chose you, then there must be a reason—a reason that transcends our logic, our knowledge, our desires, or our beliefs. This is a question of faith, no less fundamentally than whether or not you believe in a divine creator of the universe in which we live. You are part of the universe, and you are part of this world, even if you call Earth your home. You are here, now. And this world needs you. You have only your faith to tell you whether to answer the call or run away."

Thor nodded, but the conflict raged inside his mind.

Nikki and Justin woke up several hours before dawn. Even though they hadn't slept much, they felt refreshed and ready to start their day.

Nikki gave Justin a kiss and jumped out of bed first, splashed some water on her face, and started dressing. Justin joined her, feeling sad that she was covering up the perfect body that he had fallen in love with. But he knew that he loved so much more than just her body, and even when covered in leather and armor—and even the blood of their foes—she was still the ideal woman for him.

He helped her with her armor, and then she helped him, taking the time to admire his physique in the candlelight. Once they were both dressed, they straightened up the chamber, grabbed their weapons, and then crept into the hallway, trying not to wake the others.

When they reached the main floor of the residence, Nikki saw light coming from the library. She pointed and whispered, "Is someone already awake?"

"Let's find out."

Nikki and Justin entered the library, but they didn't see anyone. "Is anyone here?" Justin asked.

Nikki saw the wingback chair by the fireplace begin shaking, and she heard a muffled scream coming from the same place. She ran forward and found Bethany tied to the chair.

"Bethany! What happened?" Nikki removed the gag and started cutting the ropes with her dagger.

"Someone took Thor!" Bethany cried, rubbing her

wrists where the ropes had been. "We were in here last night, and Thor was looking for something in the journals. He came over to apologize to me for keeping me up, even though I wanted to be with him, and then four men entered room, knocked Thor unconscious, and dragged him outside. The leader tied me up and said that if we followed them or tried to free Thor, he'd kill us all."

Justin looked at Bethany, and then he said to Nikki, "Take care of her. I'll go wake the others."

Justin raced out of the library and up the stairs to the third level. He was gone for a couple of minutes, and then he returned with a tankard of water for Bethany.

"Here. Drink this," he said, handing her the tankard.

"Can you remember what the men looked like?" Nikki asked as Bethany drank.

Bethany shook her head. "They were behind me. The only one I saw was the one who tied me up. He was blond, medium height, wearing black leather trousers and jacket... oh, and he wore an eyepatch over his left eye. There were no patches or emblems on his clothing, and he was armed with a rapier and a stiletto."

"Could you tell which way they went?" Nikki asked.

Bethany gestured toward the road leading up to the top of the ridge. "It sounded like they headed that way."

Allison was the first to arrive. She made a quick examination of Bethany and found no injuries. Livvy arrived next. Peter and Kevin arrived soon after.

"What do we do?" Kevin asked after Bethany repeated her story to everyone.

"What do you think?" Nikki snapped. "We follow the trail of the men who kidnapped Thor, we rescue him and the Grand Master, and we kill anyone who tries to stop us."

The Portal of Alesia

"Can we still do that without Thor?" Allison asked.

"Of course, we can," Livvy stated confidently. "In fact, if Thor is conscious, he's fully capable of escaping on his own. We just need to be nearby to help him if he needs it. And if he's anywhere near the Grand Master, he'll find him more easily than the rest of us could."

Nikki nodded. "So when do we get started?"

"I suggest we eat first, grab enough supplies for several days, and then head out as soon as we can," Justin replied.

"I'll go saddle the horses," Kevin offered.

"I'll go with you," Peter said.

"Me, too," Justin said. "Nikki, can you organize the supplies we need? Livvy, can you and Allison get us something to eat and drink?"

Livvy and Nikki nodded.

"I can help, too," Bethany said, rising to her feet.

Livvy put her arm around Bethany's shoulder. "Come on, girls, let's head for the kitchen. And Bethany, don't worry. Thor can take care of himself, and you'll be with him again soon enough."

Chapter 5

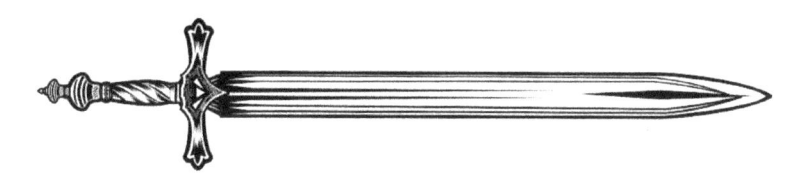

The questers led their horses away from the Grand Master's residence and up the ridge, following the road east. They were several hours away when the sun finally rose in front of them and they could safely ride their mounts.

On two separate occasions, Nikki thought she heard horses galloping in the distance, but she couldn't be certain.

"I think we could use some aerial reconnaissance," Justin suggested after Nikki mentioned to him what she had heard. "Livvy, do you think you and Kevin could fly ahead and give us an idea of what we're facing?"

"Of course." Livvy looked at Kevin. "Ready to fly with me again?"

Kevin grinned. "Always a pleasure."

Bethany was holding the reins of Thor's horse, so Peter and Nikki took the reins of Livvy and Kevin's horses. Soon, the sorceress and her mate had transformed into

The Portal of Alesia

hawks and were flying east toward the ancient buildings they had seen on their last reconnaissance.

One of the two sentries that Atreus had placed along the road from the Grand Master's residence raced to the second ancient building, where the Grand Master and Thor were being held prisoner.

"What is it," Atreus demanded when he saw the sentry approach. "I told you to watch the road."

"You also told me to inform you if anyone was heading this way. There are seven riders approaching from the west."

"Heading here?"

"Yes, sir. From the description I was given, these are the ones sent to check on the portal and find out what happened to the Grand Master and his assistants."

"Damn!" Atreus shouted. "All right. Get that extra supply wagon ready. I want the old man moved to one of the buildings east of here. I'll send over a couple of men to help you. After all, we can't risk anything happening to our prisoner, can we?"

"No, sir. Will you be going with the wagon?"

Atreus smiled. "Not yet. These interlopers have me curious. I want to capture one and squeeze some information out of him before I decide what to do next."

"Yes, sir."

Atreus mounted his horse and rode for the first building, being used as the barracks for most of his men. When he arrived, he said to them, "I need two men to help move our prisoner further east."

Two men stepped forward.

"Find the sentry preparing the supply wagon and follow his instructions."

"Yes, sir." The two men left and rode to the second building.

Turning back to the rest of the men, Atreus said, "I also need ten men to set an ambush for some riders heading here from the portal."

Ten men immediately stepped forward.

"Excellent," Atreus said. "Here's the plan..."

The two guards Atreus sent to the second building entered Boreas' cell. "Stand up, old man," one of the guards growled. "It's moving day."

They grabbed the Grand Master by his arms and pushed him down the corridor to the wagon that was waiting just outside. As he was loaded into the back of the wagon, he asked, "Where are you taking me?"

"To another one of the buildings east of here. Get comfortable back there. It's a long ride."

The two guards tied their horses to the back of the wagon and climbed onto the front deck. The sentry was waiting on his horse. He motioned for the wagon to follow him, and they started along the road heading east.

After making certain that the guards and the sentry weren't watching, Boreas looked into his shirt pocket at the mouse that was hiding there.

"Are you all right, Thor?" Boreas whispered.

The mouse nodded.

"Good thinking to change shape so quickly. I don't

want to think what would have happened had we been separated."

The mouse squeaked, and Boreas understood what it was saying. "Yes, I know you haven't made your final decision yet. But I'm still glad you're with me... in case you accept your destiny."

"What are you doing there," one of the guards yelled from the front of the wagon.

"Talking to myself," Boreas replied. "It's something old people do. If you live long enough, you may find yourself doing it, too."

"Well, knock it off," the guard barked.

Boreas looked down at the mouse and winked.

Nikki kept an eye on Livvy and Kevin as they flew east. The rest of the party was either taking care of the extra horses or were watching the trail they were following.

No one noticed the blue-colored bird that was flying parallel to them, just north of the road.

After a while, the blue bird flew away to the east.

Atreus returned to his human form in the midst of his men, who were waiting a couple of hours ahead of the questers.

"I only saw five riders, but there were eight horses," Atreus said to his men. "There's a woman warrior in their midst. She's the one I want interrogated. I'll lead her away from the others. Three of you will take her back to the barracks so I can question her. The rest of you kill the other riders and then return to the barracks. With luck, they won't notice one of their own is missing until it's too late."

The men nodded in agreement. They understood their orders... or at least they thought they did.

Livvy and Kevin saw the ancient buildings in the distance and flew toward them.

When they reached the first building, Livvy sensed several people inside. *"Twenty or so men are inside the building. They all seem to be common soldiers,"* she communicated to Kevin. *"Barely a brain between them. I guess they're the kidnapper's men."*

"Can you detect the Grand Master or Thor?" Kevin asked.

"No. Let's check the next building."

They flew to the second building, but Livvy couldn't sense anyone inside. *"It's deserted,"* she told Kevin.

"It wasn't deserted the last time we were here," Kevin noted.

"True, but it is now."

"What do we do?" Kevin asked.

"Fly east and see what or who's in the buildings east of here."

They flew east, following the road. After a few minutes, they saw a wagon ahead, being escorted by a lone horseman. As they approached the wagon, they saw two men sitting up front and an old man in the back.

"That's strange," Livvy told Kevin. *"I sense five people down there, but I only see four."*

"I only see four," Kevin confirmed. *"The one riding the*

The Portal of Alesia

horse, the two at the front of the wagon, and the one lying in the back of the wagon."

"But I still sense five," Livvy insisted.

Livvy concentrated for a moment. Then she said, "It's Thor. He shapeshifted into a mouse so he could travel with the Grand Master unseen. They're being moved to one of the buildings east of here."

"Is he all right?" Kevin asked.

"Thor is, but he says that the Grand Master is dying. His time is running out to select a successor."

"What can we do to help?" Kevin asked.

Livvy concentrated. Then she said, "Thor says to do nothing. He's got the situation under control."

"We should tell the others," Kevin suggested. "Do we follow the wagon and see which building Thor and the Grand Master are taken to, or head back now?"

"If Thor doesn't need our help, I say we head back now. I'll let him know."

Livvy concentrated again, and then she let out a cry and banked left, heading west again. Kevin followed her.

Boreas looked up when he heard the hawk's cry and saw the two birds turn and fly away to the west. Then he looked at Thor, who was still hidden in his pocket.

"Friends of yours?" he whispered.

The mouse nodded.

"Real birds or shapeshifters?"

The mouse squeaked.

"Ah, another sorcerer, like yourself. You do have interesting friends, don't you?"

The mouse squeaked again.

The wagon bounced as it drove over an exposed tree root. Boreas winced in pain. "I hope we reach our destination soon. A few more bounces like that, and I'll be dead within the hour."

As Livvy and Kevin flew west, they saw eleven men tethering their horses in a thicket near the road. The men were halfway between the first building and where Livvy and Kevin had left the others.

"That looks like an ambush," Kevin noted.

"And one of those men is different from the others," Livvy noted. "He has a brain. A malicious one, but still a brain."

She concentrated for a minute. "It's the kidnapper, and he's planning to kill us when we reach this place."

"Can we go around?" Kevin asked.

"Let's look and see if there's a way," Livvy suggested.

Livvy and Kevin flew in circles, looking for an alternate path. There wasn't one. There was nothing but dense foliage, vines, and boulders on either side of the road, making traveling off the road very difficult, if not impossible. The very thing that made traveling along the road so beautiful was also forcing them right into the trap being set by the kidnapper and his men.

"We need to let the others know," Livvy said, flying west as fast as she could. Kevin followed her.

The Portal of Alesia

Livvy and Kevin found the others next to a stream where they had stopped to water the horses. They landed in front of the others, and a moment later, they were back in their human form.

"Trouble ahead," Livvy said.

"What kind and how far?" Justin asked.

"Maybe an hour," Livvy said. "It's hard to compare flying speeds with horse speeds, but at least thirty minutes along this road. They're halfway between here and the first of the ancient buildings we saw."

"How many?" Peter asked.

"Eleven," Livvy replied. "Ten are thugs, one's the kidnapper. His men have orders to kill us all. Fortunately, he doesn't know what he's facing with us."

Livvy looked up at Nikki. "But he does have a fascination with you, Nikki. I read it in his thoughts. If I were you, I'd be extra careful."

"I'll keep her safe," Justin promised.

Livvy and Kevin got back on their horses. "So how do we handle this ambush?"

"You're sure there's no way around them?" Peter asked.

Livvy shook her head. "No. There are no paths, and the trees and boulders are too dense to take the horses through."

Justin looked east and then back at the others. "Well, if there's no choice, then we stay on the road and keep heading east. If Livvy and Kevin can let us know when we're getting close to the ambush site, we can stop just short of that point and pretend we're taking a rest break. That'll force the ambushers to leave their hiding places and come to us. Nikki and I can be in the woods and come up behind them. When they attack, well, we'll show them who they're fooling with."

"Fuck around and find out, eh?" Kevin joked.

"Exactly." Justin grinned. "Or as Thor said to me once, 'Play stupid games, win stupid prizes'."

Nikki grinned, and Kevin and Peter nodded.

"Oh, speaking of Thor," Livvy said. "We found him and the Grand Master. They're being moved to one of the ancient buildings further east. Thor says that he has things under control, but the Grand Master is dying and has to choose a successor soon."

"His assistants are all dead," Nikki reminded them. "Who is he going to choose? And doesn't the portal have to agree with the choice?"

Livvy nodded. "Thor knows that, but he wouldn't provide any details."

She glanced over at Bethany, who looked troubled.

"What's wrong, Bethany?" she asked.

"You know how fascinated Thor is with the portals, and you know that the portal spoke to him, providing him images of what happened. What if the Grand Master plans to name Thor as his successor?"

"But Thor is from earth, not this world," Kevin said. "He's going back with the rest of us once the quest is finished. He can't be a Portal Keeper... can he?"

Livvy shrugged. "I have no idea. The tavern owner could tell us, but he's not here."

"Well the Grand Master and the portal are going to have to choose someone," Allison noted. "Or we have no way to get back to the tavern. Someone has to open the portal for us. We don't know where on Annwyn Alesia is located. We don't even know what continent we're on, and if we're on a different one than Riverstone, we're screwed. It's not like we can walk or ride halfway across this world, and even if Livvy transforms us into flying beasts, we don't know in which direction to fly."

"So you're saying that Thor needs to become the Grand Master just long enough to open the portal so we can go home?" Bethany asked.

Allison shrugged. "All I'm saying is that *someone* has to open the portal for us, or we're stuck here… forever."

Bethany looked even more troubled than before. She knew that Thor had no family back on Earth to leave behind, but he had *her*, and she couldn't imagine him leaving her and staying on Annwyn.

Boreas was in distress as the wagon continued to bounce along the road.

"My time is nearly at an end, my friend," he whispered to Thor. "I need your decision now."

The mouse in his pocket squeaked.

"I know all of that," Boreas said. "But if I die before I name my successor, the Portal of Alesia will never function again. Before you reject my offer, you might want to consider this: if there's no one to operate that portal, then you and your friends are trapped here. You'll never be able to return to Riverstone without the portal; you have no other way to get there. You'll never be able to go home again."

The mouse squeaked loudly at Boreas.

"I didn't tell you because I didn't want you to make your decision with that hanging over your head. I wanted you to decide for yourself, not for what it means to your friends. But I'm out of time, and it may already be too late. I must have your answer."

The mouse stared at him for almost a minute. Then it nodded.

Boreas took the mouse in his hands and said, "I name you, Thor Larkin, as my successor to be the Keeper of the Portal of Alesia and the Grand Master of the Portal Keepers of Annwyn. All that I know, all powers that I have, I hereby pass to you. Once the transfer is complete, I will be gone. You must leave here immediately after that happens and reach the portal by nightfall. The portal will complete the process with you. Then you will be the new Portal Keeper and Grand Master. Do you understand?"

The mouse nodded.

"Very well. Let us begin."

For the next several minutes, Boreas poured all of his knowledge, memories, and power into Thor. Thor saw Boreas' life in Norway, how he came to Annwyn, and all the worlds he had explored during his nearly three-hundred-year tenure as the Grand Master.

Thor felt the unimaginable power transfer into himself, unable to fathom the extent of the magic that Portal Keepers possessed. He wondered how he could contain it all while still in the form of a field mouse.

And then it was over. Thor knew that Boreas was dead. He had completed the last task required of a Portal Keeper just in time. Now it was up to Thor to complete the process by reaching the portal before nightfall.

But there was something he needed to do first.

Thor knew he needed a different shape for his next action. He concentrated and transformed into a small

The Portal of Alesia

dragon. There was no need to transform into a larger one, since his prey was close by.

He stretched his wings and rose into the air. Without a sound, he incinerated the sentry, who was riding in front of the wagon.

The two guards in the front of the wagon saw the fire from above and turned to look. Terror froze them as they realized they were looking directly into the open mouth of an enraged dragon. They were incinerated instantly.

Thor released the two horses pulling the wagon and the two tethered to the back of the wagon. The four horses raced away from the wagon as quickly as they could.

Thor hovered over the dead Grand Master. He decided to use the wood of the wagon as a funeral pyre for the man. He ignited the wood, and let the fire send Boreas to whichever god he prayed to. He watched until the fire consumed the body of the man he was sent to save and ended up succeeding.

Knowing he had a long way to go before sunset, Thor transformed into an eagle and raced west to complete his destiny.

Bethany heard the cry of an eagle above her as the questers stopped to flush out the ambushers. She glanced upward and saw the eagle flying west. Something deep inside of her knew that it was Thor.

She didn't know how she knew, but there was no doubt in her mind that Thor had called to her as he flew toward the Portal. And it was the direction he was flying that convinced her that he and the portal were now intertwined.

"I think that was Thor that just flew over us," she whispered to Livvy.

Livvy put her arm around Bethany's shoulders. "It was. And it means that the Grand Master is dead, and Thor has gone to the portal to complete the process of becoming the new Grand Master."

Tears began running down Bethany's face. "He didn't even discuss it with me. I know our relationship is still new, but it's something we should have talked about, don't you think?"

Livvy hugged Bethany. "I believe that he wanted to, but if the Grand Master was dying, then there wasn't time. Once Thor was taken, things were set in motion that couldn't be stopped or slowed down. I don't believe for a second that he would have made this decision without you if there had been another choice. He loves you too much to do that to you. My guess? He realized that no one was getting home if he didn't agree to be the new Grand Master, so in his own way, he was taking your life into account when he made his decision. He didn't want to trap you and the rest of us here, so he agreed to trap just himself instead. He sacrificed himself for us. I can't imagine a harder or an easier choice for him to make. It was hard, because we'll be leaving him behind. It was easy, because he did what he thought was right for us... so we'd be able to go home again."

"I don't want to live without him," Bethany said, wiping the tears from her cheeks.

"Then you have a choice to make," Livvy said. "Go home with us, assuming any of us survive, or stay here with him."

The Portal of Alesia

"And give up nursing?" Bethany was shocked at the suggestion. "I'm close to being named Head Surgical Nurse. I've been working toward that for that past two years. I can't walk away now when I'm so close."

Livvy shrugged. "It's an old choice: the relationship or the job. Only you can decide which is more important."

Bethany glared at Livvy but said nothing.

Chapter 6

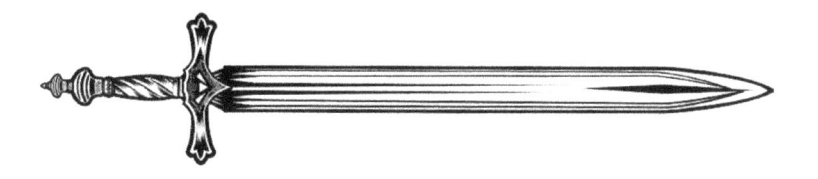

Atreus and his men waited in the thicket for the questers to ride by. After a while, he grew concerned. "They should have been here by now," he said to the sergeant next to him. "Send someone down the road and find out where they are."

"Yes, sir."

The sergeant motioned for one of the men to carry out Atreus' orders. The man slipped away and quietly made his way west along the side of the road.

The man was gone for nearly fifteen minutes. When he returned, he said, "They're resting their horses about five minutes away."

Atreus thought about this, and then he had an idea. He looked at the rest of his men. "Move out slowly, and let's see if we can catch them while they're still dismounted."

They moved forward through the woods, trying to be as quiet as possible.

The Portal of Alesia

"They're coming this way," Livvy said softly.

"They took the bait," Justin said with a smile. "Nikki and I will move around behind them. Livvy, can you protect everyone else if necessary?"

Livvy nodded.

Justin motioned for Nikki to follow him, and they moved into the woods.

Despite the dense foliage that would force horses to remain on the road, there was ample room between the trees and other plants for a person on foot to move around.

Neither Nikki nor Justin saw the blue bird circling overhead.

Atreus flew back to his men, grateful that he had decided to see for himself where the questers were.

When he changed back into his human form, he said, "I saw two trying circle around and get behind us. One of them is the one I want captured. Pretend you don't see them. I'll deal with those two myself."

He pointed to the three men he had selected to capture Nikki. "You three stay here. The rest of you know what to do."

Seven men moved forward, while Atreus crept toward Justin and Nikki.

He found them a few minutes later, hiding from the men heading toward the rest of the questers. The two were standing on either side of a massive tree that had clearly been there for centuries. He transformed into a lizard and moved toward Justin.

When he reached Justin, he transformed back into human form, only this time, he assumed the likeness of Justin. He picked up a rock and struck Justin in the back of his head. Justin started to fall, but Atreus caught him and set him carefully down on the ground so Nikki wouldn't hear. Then he crept around the tree.

Nikki was watching the men heading toward the others. Atreus tapped her on the shoulder. When she turned, he motioned for her to follow him. They left their hiding place and moved east.

After a couple of minutes, Nikki wondered why they were still moving east instead of following the kidnapper's men.

She was struck by a sudden suspicion, so she decided to try something. She and Justin both had the ability to force shapeshifters back to their original forms. If the man she was following was the kidnapper, and not Justin, she wanted to know. And if he were Justin, he would retain his present form.

Nikki concentrated, and the image of Justin changed into someone else.

Nikki drew her sword. "That's far enough. Who are you, and what have you done with my companion?"

Atreus looked surprised. "How did you...?" He looked at the clothing he was wearing, and then he smiled a wicked smile. "Ah, you have the power to force me back into my natural form. I didn't take you for a magical being, warrior girl. You're clever, but not clever enough."

Three men dressed in black stepped out of their hiding places and grabbed her roughly. One stuffed a gag into her mouth while the others took her sword and tied her wrists behind her back.

Atreus moved closer so his voice wouldn't carry. "You should be asking what I'm going to do to you, warrior girl. As for your companions, they'll all be dead shortly, so they're not really your concern anymore, are they?"

Atreus motioned for his men to follow him back to the horses.

Nikki struggled to get free, but it was no use. She was caught. Two of her captives had their swords pointed at her as they followed Atreus. She had no choice but to go with them and to whatever fate awaited her.

Her mind screamed for Justin, knowing that he'd never hear her. *Is this Atreus right? Are they already dead? Am I all alone? Oh, Justin, where are you? Please be okay.*

A few minutes later, they arrived at the thicket where the horses were tethered. "We're a horse short," Atreus observed. "Put her on mine with a bag over her head, and bring her to the barracks. I'll meet you there. Hurry. I want the information she has before the others return."

"Yes, sir."

The men put a leather bag over her head and then helped Nikki onto Atreus' horse. Her captors led her horse east at a gallop. With her hands tied behind her, she only had her legs to keep her in the saddle. She was nearly bounced off several times, but she managed to remain on the horse. She thought about escape, but she had no idea how she could get away without the use of her hands or her eyes.

Once the men had left with Nikki, Atreus transformed into the blue bird and flew east to the first ancient building.

When Nikki arrived at the building being used as the barracks for Atreus' men, she was pulled down from the horse, and the bag was removed from her head. This was the first time Nikki had seen any of the buildings, and she was surprised at its size. All thoughts of escape seemed to fade as she stared at its tan stone walls and slate-looking roof. Nikki remembered that the tavern owner said there were ten of these buildings in Alesia, and she wondered what they had been used for when they were built.

She was roughly led into the building and down the main corridor to a room that was about fifteen feet square. There were iron rings attached to the walls, and chains hanging from the ceiling. In the middle was a chair, and standing behind that chair was Atreus.

Nikki was shoved into the room.

"I don't think all that armor is necessary," Atreus said to him men. "Remove it and place it next to the door."

The men removed her armor and leathers. All that remained was her cotton shirt, her leather britches, her boots, and her undergarments. Then they forced her into the chair and tied her to it.

"You may go," Atreus said to his men. "Remain in the corridor in case I need you."

The men exited the room.

"I guess introductions are in order," he said, removing the gag from Nikki's mouth. "My name is Atreus. I am the man responsible for kidnapping the Grand Master. I'm not from Alesia, but only my men know that, since no one is supposed to be able to find Alesia who was not born here. But that's for another time. Now, who are you, and where are you from?"

Nikki remained silent. She had been through interrogation training when she was in the army, and it all came back to her: only provide name, rank, and serial number. But rank and serial number didn't apply to this situation, and she wasn't particularly interested in giving her name to a malicious kidnapper.

"Oh, come now. A name and a little background won't hurt. It's not like you're betraying a confidence, is it?"

Nikki glared at him. Then she said, "My name is Nikki. I was hired by the Keeper of the Portal of Riverstone to find out what happened to the Grand Master, and I know you came here through the portal, which means that you're from one of the Eight Realms."

Atreus' smile faded. "So you're from Riverstone. See? That wasn't so hard, was it? As for me arriving through the portal and being from one of the Eight Realms, I'd like to know how you know that. But first, tell me this. Why are you following the road to the east after you were warned that doing so would get all of you killed?"

"You have one of our companions. We want him back."

"I do?" Atreus seemed confused. "Oh, yes. I remember. The one who communicated with the portal. Yes, I ordered him to be kept away from the portal until I've finished with the Grand Master." Atreus cocked his head to one side. "So... you and your companions were willing to risk certain death just for him?" The idea seemed alien to him, and Nikki realized that Atreus had probably never been loyal to anyone other than himself before.

"Naturally."

Atreus asked several more questions, but Nikki

refused to answer.

In frustration, he opened the door and yelled for the guards. They appeared a moment later.

"Have the rest of the men returned from dealing with her companions?" he asked, gesturing toward Nikki.

"No, sir."

"What can be keeping them?" he asked himself. Then he looked at the guards. "I'm going to see what's happening. She's being uncooperative. I want to know more about her companions and the Keeper of the Portal of Riverstone. Get the information for me before I return."

"Yes, sir."

Atreus left the room, leaving the three guards behind with Nikki.

"He didn't say *how* to get the information out of her, did he, Sergeant?" one of the men asked.

The sergeant shook his head with an evil grin. "No, Corporal, he didn't. I guess we're free to use any means necessary to get what he wants."

"I'll go get the tools," the corporal offered.

"And bring us whisky, a bucket, a torch, and a fireplace poker."

The corporal looked at the sergeant wide-eyed. "Yes, Sergeant."

The two men left the room, leaving the sergeant with Nikki. "There are worse things than dying, Missy," he growled. "You're about to experience some of them. Talk, and the pain will be over quickly. Don't talk, and the pain will last until your dying breath."

Nikki said nothing, but her eyes betrayed the terror she was feeling. Despite the training she had received in the army before her first deployment—and how it tried to

The Portal of Alesia

prepare her for combat assignments in parts of the world that took pleasure in torturing and killing women in horrible ways—she knew this was real. This was happening. These weren't training instructors, they were the enemy, and the rules of war that had governed her as a soldier didn't apply on this world.

A few minutes later, the two men returned. In addition to the items the Sergeant requested, they had hammers, whips, and a variety of sharp implements that caused Nikki to start shaking involuntarily.

"I know they said that the others are dead, but I don't believe it. Between Livvy, Kevin, and Peter, none of Atreus' men should get away alive. I need to be strong and not betray my friends, no matter what's done to me."

She thought about Justin and where he was. She didn't know what had happened to him or when Atreus had changed places with him, but she prayed he was still alive.

"Tie her hands to one of the rings on the wall," the sergeant ordered.

The other two men untied Nikki from her chair and pushed her against the far wall. Her hands were raised over her head and tied to one of the iron rings. She was forced to face the wall, and her cotton shirt was lifted, exposing her back.

She heard the crack of a whip.

"You can't imagine what the whip feels like, missy," the sergeant said. "But put whisky on the tip, and it hurts ten times more."

Without warning, the whip slashed her back. She screamed in pain.

The three men laughed. "Give us the information Atreus wants, and that won't happen again. Don't, and it will happen... harder."

Nikki said nothing.

The whip slashed her, and she screamed again.

Nikki had never experienced pain like that before. She wanted to beg them to stop, to plead for relief from the agony she was experiencing at their hands, but... call it pride, warrior spirit, or just plain stubbornness, she refused to give her tormentors the satisfaction.

Nikki tried to think about anything else, other than what was happening to her. *If my companions are still alive, they'll be here soon, I need to be strong and hang on until they get here. I know they'll come for me.*

The whip struck again.

Nikki screamed, and her sobbing made her body shake.

But if these goons are right, and my companions are all dead, then joining them in death will be a relief. I've been the sole survivor before, and I swore I'd never let that happen to me again. I will not spend the rest of my life feeling guilty for still being alive. I can't go through that again.

The whip struck again, and the pain was so intense that Nikki couldn't scream. She couldn't make a sound, and her knees buckled, causing her arms and wrists to bear her full weight. Her vision was blurred from the tears that filled her eyes and streaked down her face.

She thought about Justin. *What happened to him? How did Atreus take his place without me realizing it until I was in his trap? If he's still alive, I have to endure. I have to be alive for him. But if he's dead, I don't want to live. I don't want a life that doesn't have him in it. He's my world. He's my one true love, and he's all that matters to*

The Portal of Alesia

me. *But how can I know if he's alive or dead?*

Her teeth clenched as the whip struck again.

"I can do this all day and all night, missy," the sergeant said, laughing. "Of course, we won't kill you... not yet anyway. No, we three are going to take turns with you in-between torturing you. Then we're going to let the rest of the soldiers here have *their* turn with you. What the whips don't do to your outsides, our dicks will do to your insides. And after that, we'll start using fire and the hammers. Trust me, no one will want to fuck you after that."

Nikki was sobbing uncontrollably from the pain, but she said nothing. She felt the blood running down her back, and she thought of the photos she had seen in the army of tortured women and the abuse they had been forced to endure before execution. In that moment, she welcomed death.

The sergeant grabbed her by the shoulder and spun her around. His fist struck her face. "Shut up your blubbering, missy. I can't concentrate."

Nikki couldn't stop, and the sergeant kept punching her in the face and stomach. She wanted to double over from the pain, but she couldn't. Her hands were still tied to the iron ring on the wall.

"Hey, sergeant, let us have a go at her," the corporate suggested.

"One more hit, and then it's your turn." The sergeant struck Nikki so hard that she blacked out before she could even feel the pain.

Justin regained consciousness shortly after Atreus left with

Nikki. He was face down on the ground, and his head hurt.

He leaped to his feet and looked around for her, but he couldn't find her. He did see tracks leading east, but he knew he needed to check on the others before following the tracks to see where they led.

He raced back to the others. Atreus' men had started their attack, and even though they outnumbered the questers seven to five, these men were no match for Justin's companions.

Justin saw one of Atreus' men attacking Bethany and Allison. He drew his sword and ran it through the attacker. Kevin had already killed one attacker and was about to dispatch another one. Peter was still fighting his first attacker, and Livvy was using her powers to keep the remaining attackers away from the horses.

Justin leaped toward the three men trying to get through Livvy's shield wall. He killed one of them by removing the attacker's head from his shoulders.

Peter finished killing the man he was fighting.

The two surviving attackers, realizing that they were hopelessly outnumbered by superior fighters and a sorceress, dropped their swords.

Livvy walked up to them, staring intently at them for a minute. Then she snapped her fingers, and the two men dropped to the ground with a surprised expression on their dead faces.

"What did you do?" Kevin asked.

"I stopped their hearts," she replied coldly. Turning to Justin, she said, "They have Nikki. They took her to their barracks, which is the first of the ancient buildings just east of here. Atreus wanted to interrogate her while his men were killing us. But knowing Nikki, she won't cooperate."

The Portal of Alesia

"We need to go after her," Justin said.

Everyone mounted their horses and rode east. A blue bird circled them and then flew off toward the barracks.

Atreus watched the last of his men get killed by Nikki's companions. He wanted to race back to the barracks and get the rest of his men, but if these six could defeat his men so easily, he wasn't sure he had enough men in the barracks to stop them. And since one of them was clearly a sorcerer, he wasn't sure he'd survive the encounter either.

Then he remembered the Grand Master. *"I only sent him away with three guards. They're no match for this bunch. I need to go after them and help find a better hiding place. That old man is getting close to his death, and I need to be there, so I can receive his powers."*

He flew back to the barracks, transformed into human form, mounted his horse—which had been used to bring Nikki for interrogation—and raced down the road to the east.

He had no idea that Boreas was already dead, and he had completely forgotten about Nikki.

Justin and the others rode past the thicket and saw the horses left there by Atreus' men. They kept riding.

When they reached the barracks, Livvy informed Justin that Nikki was inside, but unconscious, and there were at least twenty of Atreus' men inside.

Justin, Kevin, and Peter entered the barracks first.

They saw the long corridor and torchlight at the far end. The sound of men's voices talking and laughing also came from the end of the corridor.

They started forward, but then they saw a door open. Three men exited and closed the door behind them.

"She'll be out for a while," one of the men said. "Let's join the others for some food before round two begins."

"Did you have to hit her so hard?" another one of the men asked.

"She had it coming," the first man responded. "Maybe she'll remember that when we start questioning her again."

The three men disappeared down the corridor. Livvy, Bethany, and Allison entered the barracks. Justin motioned for them to stay where they were while he, Kevin, and Peter looked for Nikki.

They started with the room the three men had just exited.

Nikki was sitting in the chair in the middle of the room. Her hands were tied behind her, and a rope at her waist kept her seated. She was slumped over and unconscious. Her shirt was red in the back from where she was bleeding in several places.

Justin was horrified at what he saw. "Nikki!" he cried. She didn't respond. He raced forward and knelt next to her. He pushed the hair away from her face and saw the bruising and the cuts above her left eye and on her lips.

"My god, what have they done to you?" There was no need to ask who had done this to her. He knew. When he looked around the room, he saw the implements of torture they had used, including the leather whip with blood dripping from its tip.

Two conflicting emotions ripped through him. He felt

rage for what those three men had done to Nikki. But he also felt profound guilt. *I was supposed to have your back. I was supposed to protect you. I made a promise, and I didn't keep it.* He gently touched her back and looked at her blood on his hand. *Look at what they've done to you. It's my fault. I should be the one tied to this chair, not you. I should have been more alert. I should have kept my promise to you.*

Justin went cold inside and the rage and guilt stripped away his humanity and compassion. The desire to kill was all that remained. He wiped her blood on his face, as if he wanted her spirit to be part of him.

"Peter, go get the girls," he said in a voice like ice. "And tell Bethany and Allison to bring all of their medical supplies."

Peter, unprepared for the sudden change in Justin, left the room without a word. He returned a minute later with Livvy, Bethany and Allison.

Justin felt the beast within him battling to be set free. It wanted to be unleashed, and he wanted to let it out. He stood, faced Bethany and Allison, and icily demanded, "Do what you can for her. I'll be back shortly."

Justin exited the room. Kevin and Peter looked at each other, and then they followed Justin out the door and toward the torch-lit room at the end of the corridor.

Justin didn't draw his sword, and he didn't slow down. He entered the great hall at the far end of the corridor. Once Peter and Kevin had entered, he closed and locked the door behind them. He turned and let out a roar that chilled the hearts of the twenty men eating and drinking inside, and then he let the beast within him take over completely.

With his bare hands, Justin went on a murderous rampage the likes of which no one in the room had ever seen before. He killed anyone within reach. Eight were dead before any of the men had the sense to draw their weapons, but it was too late for that.

Justin didn't stop. He didn't draw or grab a weapon. He didn't consider what he was doing. He simply snapped necks and ripped out the throats of anyone in his way.

Peter and Kevin had their swords drawn, but Justin hadn't left anyone for them.

Justin saw the three men who had exited the room where he found Nikki. His bloodlust went into overdrive as he leapt for them. He grabbed the corporal by his neck and twisted his head off like a chicken's. A blow to the head killed the man next to the corporal, leaving only the sergeant still alive and standing.

The sergeant took one look at Justin's face and saw his own death coming for him. He tried to draw his dagger, but Justin snatched it from his hand and proceeded to disembowel the sergeant.

"Mercy," the sergeant cried, trying to keep his insides from spilling out all over the floor.

"No," was Justin's only reply. "This is for Nichole." He slashed the sergeant across his throat, sending blood spraying everywhere as the sergeant's blood and bowls escaped from his body. Justin watched dispassionately, and then he turned away. In a sudden movement, he turned back, threw the dagger at the sergeant, and watched it stick in his chest, piercing the man's heart.

Justin walked over to the water barrel by the door, washed off the blood, and headed back to the room where they had found Nikki.

The Portal of Alesia

Kevin and Peter put away their swords and followed him. Neither had seen Justin in full berserker mode like this before, but then again, they had never seen the woman Justin loved after she had been tortured.

Bethany and Allison were working on Nikki when Justin returned. She was unconscious, and they had her lying on a blanket on the floor. Her face was deathly pale.

"How is she?" Justin asked, kneeling next to her.

"She's going to need a lot of stitches," Bethany said. "Her lip and the cut above her eye will need them, and it's possible that her back will need them, too. I won't know until I can get medicated plaster on her to seal the wounds. It'll take several hours to finish, and then she can't be moved for at least two days—possibly longer."

"Two days? She's hurt that bad?"

Bethany nodded. "If we hadn't gotten here when we did, she'd be dead within the hour."

Justin's eyes began to water. He looked up at Livvy. "Isn't there anything you can do?"

"I'm doing it," she said. "I'm keeping her unconscious so she won't feel any pain while Bethany and Allison work on her, and I'm keeping her heart beating so she won't die. She's a tough girl, that's for sure, but what they did to her.... no one's that tough."

Justin nodded, too choked up to say anything. Then he glanced over at the implements of torture the three men had used—or were intending to use—on Nikki. He stood, grabbed them, ran out of the building, and hurled them into the dense brush. When he returned to the building and entered the corridor to be with Nikki, he let out a roar of both rage and anguish, brought on by the guilt he felt. He fell to his knees and began weeping inconsolably.

"*Dear God, if you have to take someone, take me. Spare Nichole. Please. This is my fault. I failed her. I made her a promise, and I didn't keep it. I was supposed to have her back. I was supposed to protect her. But thanks to my own stupidity, she's hanging on by a thread. Don't punish her for my mistake. And if she is to be called home to you, then let me die in battle so I can be with her. Don't make me live with the shame of knowing that I didn't prevent her death. I'll do anything you ask if you'll grant me this one request.*"

CHAPTER 7

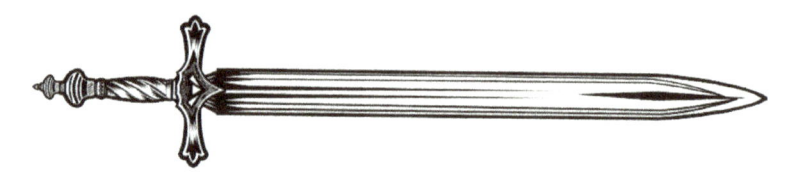

As Atreus rode east, he thought about how his perfect plan was beginning to unravel. Boreas's health was failing faster than expected, a sorcerer and the portal had communicated with each other, someone from Riverstone sent a team to find out what had happened to the Grand Master, and now those people were killing his men like they had no fighting skills at all. Nothing was going as planned, and he was not happy.

After a couple of hours, he reached the charred remains of the wagon carrying Boreas to his new prison. The bones of three people were visible in the ashes. Nearby, there were more ashes, mixed with the bones of a man and a horse.

"Three guards and the prisoner," Atreus muttered to himself. "So the Grand Master is dead, and his power died with him. Now I'll never get control of the Portal of Alesia. The Princess will be pissed that I failed my mission. I wonder what manner of execution she'll choose. She was quite explicit about the price of failure."

Atreus was about to turn around when a thought struck him. "Why are the guards dead? Why is everything burned?"

He dismounted and examined the ashes. He picked up a handful and sniffed it. "Dragon fire! But there aren't any dragons in this part of the world." But there was no mistaking the smell. A dragon had incinerated Boreas and the three men escorting him east.

A gnawing suspicion overtook him. "That sorcerer. Somehow he was here." He thought back to the instructions he gave the soldiers who captured Thor. "I'm an idiot! I told them to keep the sorcerer away from me and from the portal. I thought I'd be with Boreas until the end, but I wasn't. Those fools took the sorcerer to the same building where Boreas was being held. And once Boreas found out that the portal had spoken to the sorcerer, the Grand Master had found his successor. That means the sorcerer is the new Grand Master of the Portal Keepers."

"Unless..."

Atreus remembered what he had learned about passing the powers from one Portal Keeper to another. "Boreas must have passed his powers to the sorcerer, but the sorcerer must then bond with the portal itself before he can be the true successor. If I can reach the portal before he does, I might be able to stop him. Then the portal will die, which is a better outcome than someone the Princess can't control being the new Grand Master."

Atreus, knowing that the sorcerer had a huge head start, transformed into a falcon and headed west toward the portal. His horse turned and trotted after its rider.

Atreus reached the barracks very quickly, and he decided to check on his men before continuing to the portal. He wanted to know if they had brought the sorcerer to the same building where the Grand Master was being held.

He landed and transformed into his human form. But when he entered the barracks, he couldn't hear his men. He did hear the voices of the sorcerer's companions.

Atreus quickly transformed into a wasp and flew toward the voices.

"I know they defeated the men I sent to ambush them after I captured that warrior girl. But what are they doing here? And where are the rest of my men?"

He flew by the open door and saw Nikki lying on the floor, surrounded by Bethany, Allison, and Livvy. She looked dead to him—he didn't know the others were doing all they could to save Nikki's life.

"The fools! The stupid, stupid fools! They tortured her to death. I never told them to torture her. I never told them not to, but it's not something they should have done without checking with me first. And to kill her... that was a foolish mistake. I'll skin them alive myself when I get my hands on them."

Atreus continued looking for his men. He flew down the corridor to the great hall. There he found the remains of his men. He darted across the room, looking at the savagery used to kill them all.

"Throats ripped out, necks snapped like twigs, that fool sergeant disemboweled... The sorcerer's companions must have been enraged when they found that one of their own—a woman at that—had been so brutally murdered.

At least I don't have to deal with the fools who killed her. I wonder if they got any information from her before they killed her. Now that they're dead, I'll never know."

Sickened by the sight, he flew outside, transformed back into a falcon, and headed west as fast as he could fly.

Thor reached the portal well-before sunset. The only sound he heard was the wind in the trees, but as he approached the portal, he heard the music in his mind.

He knew what he had to do, but he wasn't sure how he knew it. He landed in front of the portal and transformed back into his human form.

He could sense anticipation coming from the portal as he approached the ancient structure. He stepped inside and reached out.

He was suddenly surrounded by silver light, shimmering like a waterfall all around him. The familiar music began to change. There was so much more richness to the sound, now that he had received Boreas' powers and was prepared to listen.

The portal spoke directly to his mind, not in images as before, but in ways that Thor could easily understand. The entire history and purpose of the portal opened up to him, as he became one with his destiny.

From the dawn of time, this had been Thor's purpose. It wasn't that he was in the right place at the right time, it's that the universe saw to it that he was where he needed to be when he needed to be there. The millions and millions of decisions and actions across the eons that were necessary to bring him to this moment in time and space

The Portal of Alesia

were staggering, and he saw the ancient portal builders not just as simple explorers but as emissaries of the universe's ultimate purpose—bringing all life together.

He also saw something unexpected. Not one of the Grand Masters had ever been born on Annwyn. The first Grand Master had been one of the visiting beings who created the portals and remained behind when his companions left for other worlds. The rest had been from Earth, having been brought to Annwyn at various times throughout the ages.

The deepest inner workings of the portals were opened to Thor, and he understood exactly how to use its indescribable power. He understood how the Portal of Alesia and the Portal of Riverstone created temporary portals so it was possible to travel between worlds and back again. The physics behind the portals, so complex, seemed so simple now that the portal had explained it to him.

It seemed like he had been inside the portal for weeks, but in fact, he had only been inside for a few minutes.

When the portal had finished sharing its knowledge and power with Thor, the silver light faded away. Only the music remained—powerful and joyous, celebrating the arrival of the new Keeper.

Thor saw people approaching from the villages and farms that lay to the west. He stepped out of the portal to greet them.

Alesia had a very small population, but they were friendly people. They looked at the Grand Master as their leader, even though the Grand Masters had rarely gotten involved in the political issues of the villages. The people of Alesia saw it as their great privilege to serve the needs of the Grand Master and his assistants—most of whom had grown up nearby.

Thor walked toward the people, who bowed in greeting to the new Grand Master.

"My name is Thor," he said to the assembly. "It is my great pleasure to be among you."

"The pleasure is ours, Grand Master," one of the older gentlemen said. "We are your neighbors, and we are your servants. Anything you need, you have but to ask. We will bring you food, fuel for your fire, and people to help you maintain your residence. It is our purpose and our joy."

The man gestured toward five young men. "We have selected these men to be your assistants. If they are not suitable, just let us know what you need, and we will provide it."

Thor smiled and bowed as he recited the ancient words used by every Grand Master before him. "I thank you for your generous gifts and offers. I am new here, but the memories of all who came before me are part of me now, so I feel as though I have lived among you since the dawn of time. Your names are all known to me. I take these men as my assistants, and I grieve with you at what happened to their predecessors. Boreas has passed beyond to be with his assistants, and his successor was there when needed, as it has been since the beginning, and as it will be until the end."

The assembly bowed, and the older gentleman signaled to four wagons that had stopped some distance away. They rode forward.

"Here are provisions for you and your assistants, as well as the team that will come twice a week to wash and clean for you. Your residence has been empty for several days, and a good cleaning is overdue, yes?"

The Portal of Alesia

Thor nodded. "I appreciate your thoughtfulness and thoroughness. Will you and your neighbors join me for supper?"

The older man smiled and shook his head. "This is the time for you and your assistants to get acquainted. There will be many other opportunities for us to spend time together, Grand Master."

Thor nodded, and he and the assistants followed the wagons up to his home on the ridge.

He didn't notice the falcon perched on a nearby tree branch, watching all that had happened.

After the supplies had been put away and the house cleaning had begun, Thor assigned quarters for his assistants. Then he went to the library and began straightening up the mess left behind the night he had been kidnapped by Atreus.

He wanted to rejoin his companions to track down and deal with Atreus and his men, but Thor knew that wasn't possible. He needed to assign duties to his assistants, and then he needed to convene a council of the other Portal Keepers. These tasks would tie him up for at least a full day.

As he sat at his desk, he reached his thoughts out to Livvy. *"Livvy, can you hear me?"*

"Yes, I can. Thor?"

"It's me. What's going on?"

"We're at the first building east of you. It's what Atreus' men were using for a barracks. It's just us here now... alive anyway."

"I was held in the second building. That's where I met my predecessor."

"Ahhh," Livvy said. "So it's true. You're the new Grand Master. Bethany won't be thrilled to hear that."

"There's nothing I could do about it. It was... necessary. She and I will need to have a long talk before y'all head back to Riverstone and then home."

"A very long talk," Livvy agreed.

"What happened to Atreus' men?" Thor asked.

"Justin happened. He unleashed that beast he keeps chained up inside of him. Kevin and Peter said he slaughtered all twenty of Atreus' soldiers with his bare hands. I guess it's understandable, after what happened to Nikki?"

"What do you mean, 'what happened to Nikki'?" Thor demanded.

"Atreus' men tortured her, Thor. She was whipped and beaten. She's barely alive, and I'm not sure if Bethany, Allison, and I have what it takes to save her."

"What about your ability to resurrect?" Thor asked.

"I thought about that, but it won't work in this case. Her body is too broken. If she dies, and I resurrect her back into this body, she'll just die again, and then I'll never be able to bring her back. I think we may have to send her home and hope that, as the tavern owner said, what happens on a quest really does remain with the quest. Otherwise, we'll lose two of the team instead of just you."

"I wish I could be there to help," Thor said, "but the portal needs me here. And there's still Atreus to deal with. I don't know if he intends to complete his mission, or if he's going to abandon it, but I can't let any plan of his succeed, no matter the cost."

The Portal of Alesia

He hesitated for a moment. *"It might be better to send you all home now. I don't think there's anything else you can do, all things considered."*

"Nikki can't be moved yet," Livvy said. *"If she lives, and if she stabilizes in the next few days, we can try to move her then, but not now."*

"I could always open a portal there and bring you here," Thor said. *"Or I can open a portal there and send you directly to the tavern at Riverstone. The tavern owner could get you all home without having to move Nikki much—only a few steps into the portal I create. Come to think of it, I could open a portal there and send you directly back home, but I'd need to get with the tavern owner to understand how he plays with time so it only seems like you were gone for a few hours, instead of weeks. I understand the principle, but I want someone who has done it before to make sure I don't screw it up."*

Livvy thought about this. *"That could work, but right now, she wouldn't survive even that. Check in with me tomorrow, and we can talk about it some more. For now, we're going to make ourselves at home here and see what happens with her recovery."*

"Okay," Thor conceded. Then he thought of something. *"Is Justin okay? I've seen him after he's unleashed the beast before, and if he took on twenty men barehanded, he's probably a wreck inside."*

"You have no idea," Livvy said. *"He blames himself for what happened to Nikki. For some reason, he feels guilty that he didn't protect her. It's survivor's guilt on a scale I've never seen before. And if she dies, I don't want to think about how far over the edge that could push him."*

"I wish there was something I could do for him, but

it's all up to Nikki now, isn't it?"

"Yes," Livvy confirmed.

"Okay. I'll reach out to you tomorrow. Give everyone my best. I'll pray for Nikki."

"Thanks, Thor."

Livvy broke the connection, and Thor leaned back in his chair, deeply disturbed that one of his companions was dying and another one was in mental anguish over it.

Atreus waited until the portal was deserted. He tried to approach it, but an invisible barrier prevented him from reaching it. *A shield wall? What do you expect from a sorcerer who becomes a Portal Keeper?*

He transformed back into a falcon and flew toward the Grand Master's residence. He encountered another shield wall, keeping him from the house and the clearing around the house. *Damn! So much for slipping a knife between his ribs. What do I do now?*

Atreus flew to one of the tallest trees and landed on the top branch, watching the rising moon cast its bluish light around the residence and the portal.

"If I kill the new Grand Master, it'll solve one problem, but it'll cause another one. Plus I don't know how you kill a sorcerer. Besides, Princess Telise wants control of the portals, not to watch the portals shut down one-by-one until none of them functional anymore. So to keep from going back to her and telling her that I failed, I need to figure out a way to force the Grand Master to surrender his powers to me."

"But how do I do that?

The Portal of Alesia

He thought about it until he saw the locals, who had brought the food and came to clean the residence, heading back to their villages.

"What if... no. Threatening the villagers wouldn't make him surrender his powers. He doesn't really know them, and they'd never let him sacrifice himself to save them. They'd consider it an honor to die in his service."

Atreus watched the wagons making their way west.

The wagons reminded him of the incinerated remains he encountered on the road heading east. That made him think back to what he discovered at the barracks—his men dead, the warrior girl dead, and her companions now occupying the building.

"His companions! If the surviving six of them were threatened, he might surrender his powers to keep them safe. They're his friends, and he already knows that my men killed one of them. He'll take me seriously if I threated to kill more of them. And who knows? Maybe one of them is more than just a friend."

"But I don't have any men, and I can't take them without help." He looked at the wagons disappear into the distance. "And the locals won't help me. I guess I'll need to go back to Princess Telise and tell her I need more men. Better men this time. Men who obey orders, instead of acting stupidly and messing up all of my plans. At least I can blame my failures on the men she originally sent with me. None are left to contradict me."

Knowing it was a long flight to Princess Telise and the High King's realm, Atreus transformed himself into a great eagle and flew off to the south, hoping he was heading in the right direction.

Bethany and Livvy were stretched out on the floor next to Nikki, in case she needed anything during the night. They were lying on their bedrolls and using their blankets as pillows. Nikki was still unconscious.

Justin stood guard just inside the main entrance of the building. He didn't move, he didn't speak, and he barely ate or drank. He just stood there like a statue.

As Kevin watched his employee and closest friend from across the room, he mentally wrestled with four different issues while he tried to remain awake. First, he was concerned about the way Justin had reacted to finding Nikki at death's door—slaughtering all of Atreus' men barehanded.

Second, Kevin was worried about what Justin might do if Nikki died, and there were no more of Atreus' thugs upon whom he could take out his grief.

Third, Kevin was worried about Bethany. It was clear that something had happened with Thor that was going to impact his relationship with Bethany substantially, but Kevin didn't really understand what it was, other than Bethany felt betrayed by something Thor had done.

And fourth, Kevin worried about his own relationship with Livvy. She was carrying a heavy burden as the only sorcerer still on the team, and the effort she was expending to save Nikki was draining her powers, in spite of her ability to recharge her powers immediately ten times during the quest. The ten times were almost used up, and if her powers failed when needed the most, there was no telling what could happen to the rest of the team.

And Kevin was helpless to do anything for Livvy... or

Bethany, or Justin.

As he struggled with his thoughts, Kevin realized how completely he loved Livvy and how much he depended on her. The last thing he wanted was to lose her now, but if Nikki died, and Livvy blamed herself, Kevin could see her pulling away in her grief and shame.

Kevin shook his head to clear those thoughts. *No sense worrying about what hasn't happened yet. There's plenty to worry about without searching for more things.*

Peter and Allison were sitting next to each other with their backs to the wall, watching Nikki. Neither could sleep, so Peter stood and held out his hand to Allison. She looked up at him with a curious look. He gestured toward the corridor, and she nodded and took his hand.

They crept out of the room and down the corridor away from Justin and Kevin. They came to a room that looked like it was the quarters for one of the officers. They slipped inside.

The floor was covered with a large burgundy rug that had an intricate pattern on it. There was a desk next to the bed, a small bookcase, and a round table near the door. Other than that, the room was bare, like the other rooms in the building. Nothing hung on the walls or from the ceiling. The only light available was from candles sitting on the furniture around the room.

Peter lit the candles on the table, closed the door, and gestured for Allison to sit down. She did, and he sat in the chair next to her.

"Do you mind if we talk?" Peter asked.

"About what?" Allison responded.

Peter seemed to be at a loss for words. "About what's going on," he said, finally. "About what's happening between Justin and Nikki, between Thor and Bethany, between Kevin and Livvy..." He looked into Allison's eyes. "Are we okay?"

Allison put her hand on Peter's. "Of course we're okay," she said. "Why would you think we have a problem, just because everyone else seems to be having problems?"

"Because everyone else seems to be having problems," Peter replied. "And I want to make certain that I'm... we're doing everything possible to keep their problems from causing problems between us."

Allison leaned forward, her face close to Peter's. "Listen to me, Peter Jordan. We are okay."

Peter looked relieved. "I'm glad to hear that, Allison Maccabe, because I love you. I've wanted to tell you for a long time, but there never seemed to be a proper moment to say anything."

Allison's eyes lit up, and she smiled. "I love you, too. And we're going to get through this, and we're going to go home, and we're going to build a new life together. Got it?"

"Got it."

They wanted to make love, but if Nikki needed something, Allison had to be ready to come to her aid immediately. Peter understood, so they held hands and talked about the kind of future they wanted together until the candles had melted all over the tabletop.

But the longer they talked, the more they wanted to be physically connected. Finally, Allison whispered, "I can't stand it anymore. Quickie?"

Peter nodded. Allison stood and hiked up her skirt,

The Portal of Alesia

removing her undergarment. Peter, who remained in his seat, pulled down his pants, revealing that he was already fully erect. Allison reached for him and stimulated him with her hand as he reached between her legs to stimulate her. She was already quite wet.

She moved forward and guided him inside of her as she sat on him. She clutched the back of his chair as his hands clutched her hips, keeping the skirt of her dress out of the way.

She moved up and down on him, giving her legs a workout as he penetrated her deeply. She let go of the chair with one hand and grabbed Peter by the back of the head, kissing him as she continued moving up and down on him. Faster and faster she moved, enjoying the sensations of him being deep inside of her. She kept her eyes open, never taking her gaze off of his face. Then she orgasmed, and a moment later, she felt him release inside of her. She giggled as she felt the warm liquid shooting into her, something that Peter had gotten used to and had come to enjoy when they made love. It was amazing to him the pleasure she derived from that one aspect of their lovemaking.

She sat on him and wrapped both of her arms around his neck and shoulders, kissing him and holding him tightly.

When she finally stood, she walked over to the bed, pulled off the sheet, and used it to clean herself. Then she handed it to Peter so he could clean himself. She pulled on her undergarment, straightened her skirt, and sat down in the chair next to him.

Peter cleaned himself, tossed the soiled sheet back onto the bed, and pulled his pants back up. Then he looked at Allison, held out his hand, and she took it.

"What else do we need to talk about?" she asked, resting her head on his shoulder.

Chapter 8

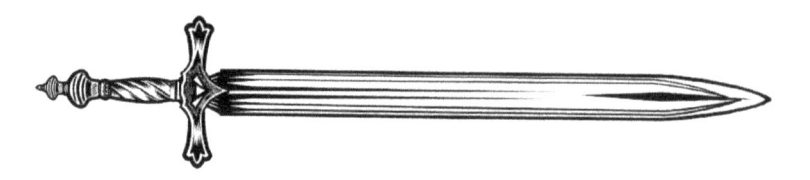

Thor met with the other Portal Keepers the day after he bonded with the Portal of Alesia. As the Grand Master of the Portal Keepers of Annwyn, it was important for him to meet them and for them to meet him.

The meeting was held in the Grand Master's residence shortly after noon. They met in the library, which had been straightened up by Thor, his assistants, and the villagers who came to clean the residence the night before.

After Thor introduced himself, he shared how he had become the new Grand Master and what had happened to Boreas. Most of the Portal Keepers accepted the news calmly. One looked decidedly uncomfortable after learning that Atreus was the kidnapper—and that he and his men weren't from Alesia—something that Boreas had shared with Thor during their captivity. When Thor mentioned that the portal had shown him Atreus and his men arriving via the portal in the middle of the night, the one portal keeper began sweating.

"It's clear to me that they arrived in Alesia from one of the Eight Realms," Thor said after he told his story. "There's no other way. No one could fly here, and even if Atreus and his men were all shapeshifters, they don't know where here is. The only people who do know where here is are the people in this room. Alesia doesn't appear on any map, except for the map that shows the locations of the portals, which only *we* are allowed to see. Also, no one could sail here, even if this world had ocean-going ships, because, again, no one knows where here is. No, what the portal showed me was the truth. Atreus and his men came through the portal, and if they've done it once, they could do it again."

Thor looked around the room, and his eyes rested on the one Portal Keeper who appeared uncomfortable and kept his gaze on the floor in front of him. "Essien, tell me again which portal you keep."

Essien's face turned a deep shade of red. He cleared his throat, then cleared it again before looking up at Thor. "The portal of the High Kingdom, Grand Master."

"And why are you so uncomfortable, Essien? You appear to be a man with something to hide."

Essien stammered, but provided no intelligible answer.

Thor looked around the room. "Did any of you use your portals to send people to Alesia?"

The tavern owner raised his hand. "I did, Grand Master." The tavern owner smiled.

Thor grinned. "Yes, Ravana, I know you sent eight people here a few days ago. Did you send anyone else?"

"No, Grand Master."

"Did any of the rest of you?"

The Portal of Alesia

Everyone except for Essien replied that they hadn't.

Thor turned his attention to Essien again. "That leaves you, Essien."

Essien looked like he was going to cry. "Grand Master, I did send people through the portal to here, but that was more than a month ago. The High King's niece, Princess Telise, sent a delegation to speak with your predecessor. It happens from time to time, so I didn't think anything of it. It never occurred to me that there could be a link between that delegation and Boreas' kidnapping."

"And you didn't grow suspicious when the delegation never returned?"

"It's not uncommon for me not to see when people *arrive* through my portal, Grand Master. I'm only needed to open the portal to *send* someone through. Boreas, and now you, can open your portal and send people to the High Kingdom's realm at any time. I just assumed that the delegation returned that way without notifying me they were back, and I thought nothing more about them."

"And now that you know they kidnapped Boreas and attempted to force him to name Atreus as his successor?"

"Grand Master, I'm mortified that I may have unwittingly played a part in what happened with your predecessor. Atreus seemed like a decent sort, and I've never had to question Princess Telise's requests or motives before."

"And are you not in possession of a map that shows the location of Alesia?" Thor asked.

"I am Grand Master. We all are. But I don't believe that Princess Telise is."

"Have you ever shown anyone your map?"

Essien's face turned red. "It's... possible that Princess

Telise may have seen the map... on occasions."

The other Portal Keepers began shouting angrily at this news. Thor had to stand to make them quiet down.

"What can you tell me about this Princess?" Thor asked, leaning forward with his fists on the table. He was still trying to decide if Essien had been completely honest or not.

"She and her half-sister, Angélique, are the only living relatives of High King Constantine of the Eight Realms. The oldest of the two, Princess Angélique, is a warrior, and she commands the two armies of the High King. Princess Telise is a... politician, like her uncle. King Constantine is... well..."

"A corrupt old fool who loves intrigue and debauchery more than he loves his people or governing the Eight Realms, which he leaves mostly to the Princesses Telise and Angélique," Ravana, the tavern owner and Keeper of the Portal of Riverstone interrupted. "His excesses are legendary, if not a bit exotic, and Princess Telise is his favorite, becoming more like him every day. At least Princess Angélique understands duty, and she'll make an excellent High Queen when King Constantine either steps aside or dies. Personally, I wouldn't trust Princess Telise as far as I could throw this building."

"You malign the young Princess, Ravana," Essien protested. "I have always found her to be a sweet and honest child."

"Around you, perhaps," the Keeper of the Portal of Cockaigne interjected, "but I find her to be a power-hungry little imp who delights in running errands for her uncle when he needs deniability. Needless to say, she now runs most of his errands for him."

Several of the other Portal Keepers shared their impressions of Princess Telise and her uncle, and none of their characterizations were positive.

Essien looked around the room with a bewildered look on his face. "My brothers, I trust each of you with my life, and if this is what you've seen and experienced, then all I can say is that she is very different around me than she is around each of you. I have seen no evidence of the person you have described."

"And how did she come to see a map with the location of Alesia on it?" Thor asked in a tone that made Essien's spine shiver.

Essien turned red again. "She may have pieced it together... from me. Grand Master, she and I talk all the time. She asks questions, and I try to answer. While I never gave her the exact location of Alesia, she may have pieced together from other things I told her over the years."

"So your carelessness has exposed the location of the one place that no one outside of this room is supposed to know? And it never occurred to you that someone might use that information for their own personal gain?"

Essien shook his head but remained silent.

"I think we've learned a few things here today," Thor said, taking his seat. "Atreus and his men were sent through the portal several weeks ago, and you were told they were coming here for one purpose, when in fact it was for a very different and sinister purpose. Is it fair to say that the next time she or someone in the Royal Court requests to send someone here, you'll investigate the legitimacy of the request more strongly to make certain that there's no deceit involved?"

"Yes, Grand Master," Essien affirmed.

After the meeting with the Portal Keepers was concluded, and the Keepers of the portals in the Eight Realms had been sent back to their homes, Thor and Ravana talked in private.

"Nikki was tortured by Atreus' men and is clinging to life by a thread," Thor told the tavern owner. "When you sent us home after the last quest, all of our wounds vanished. Would that happen again if we sent Nikki home through the portal? Would her injuries vanish like they had never happened, returning her to health immediately?"

Ravana nodded. "Yes, Grand Master. Her body would return there just as it was when she left. There would be no physical ill effects from her time here. I can't speak for the mental effects, however."

"Livvy is worried about moving her in her present condition. How can we get her home if we can't bring her to one of the portals?"

Ravana looked shocked. "Just how did they torture her to create this kind of problem?"

"According to Livvy, they whipped her and then beat her. It was brutal, that's for certain."

Ravana shook his head in disgust. "And that fool Essien let those soldiers come here—the one place on this world where nothing bad is ever supposed to happen. This place was established as the heart and soul of this world. That's why its location remains secret, so no corruption can ever come here. And he just let them through without a second thought."

"Essien's fate is for another time. Right now, my focus

The Portal of Alesia

is on saving Nikki's life."

The tavern owner thought about it for a moment. "The problem is getting Nikki from where she is now to my portal, right?"

Thor nodded. "Is there any way I can create a temporary portal where she is now, like the one you created when you brought us here, that will allow me to send her directly to Riverstone? Once inside the tavern, you can send her home without moving her, right?"

"You could create a temporary portal that links the tavern with wherever she is now. Once she's in the tavern, you can... *remove* the temporary portal, and I can send her home. I can use the game to make certain that she arrives safely and that she's physically well. Are you going to send the others home with her? The quest is technically completed."

"All except for the shapeshifter, Atreus," Thor said. "He's still out there somewhere, and I don't need him coming after me like he did Boreas."

"Yes, but you're a sorcerer, Grand Master," the tavern owner reminded him. "And you're even more powerful now. What can he do to you?"

"Didn't you ask yourself the same questions when Boreas disappeared and his assistants were murdered?" Thor inquired. "He still wants control of this portal, either for himself or on behalf of another. As long as he is still pursuing that goal, there's no telling what he might do. I'd like to keep the rest of the questers here. I could send one of them back with Nikki, but not all of them."

The tavern owner nodded. "I'll head back to Riverstone and prepare to receive Nikki. I'll let you know when she's home safe and if her wounds are healed."

Thor held out his hand. "Thank you, my friend."

"My pleasure, Grand Master."

"She's conscious," Bethany said to Livvy.

"Nikki's awake?" Livvy exclaimed.

Bethany nodded. "She weak, and she's in pain, but she seems lucid enough to know what's going on."

"Does this mean that she's okay?"

Bethany hesitated, looking down.

"What aren't you telling me?" Livvy demanded.

"She's dying," Bethany admitted. "She needs a trauma center, not this crude medieval medicine that we're able to practice here. I don't think she'll make it to sunrise."

Livvy's hand flew up and covered her mouth. Then she said, "Does Justin know?"

Bethany shook her head.

"Well, he needs to know. Now."

Bethany nodded and went to find Justin.

"Livvy, can you hear me? It's Thor."

"Thor, I can hear you. Nikki's awake, but she's dying. Bethany says she won't make it to sunrise."

"We're sending her home immediately," Thor said. *"I'm creating a temporary portal to send her from there to Riverstone. The tavern owner will get her home from there. No one will have to move her. I do want someone to go with her—either Bethany or Allison. Everyone else needs to leave the building until Nikki is in Riverstone."*

"How long before you're ready to send her?" Livvy asked.

"Thirty minutes," Thor said. Then explained why the

The Portal of Alesia

rest of the questers weren't going home and why he felt that Nikki and whoever went home with her would both be coming back once it was confirmed that Nikki was all right.

Livvy understood. *"Okay. We'll be ready."*

Thor broke the connection, and Livvy went to find Bethany and Allison.

Justin was kneeling next to Nikki when Livvy arrived. She motioned for Bethany and Allison to follow her. She wanted to talk to them, and she wanted to give Justin his privacy with Nikki, in case this was the last time they spoke.

Once in the corridor, Livvy explained what Thor and the tavern owner were doing.

"And they think this will heal her?" Bethany asked.

"It worked last time. Thor seems confident that it'll work. It's creating the temporary portal that had him unsure the last time I talked with him."

"And he wants one of us to go back with her?" Allison said.

Livvy nodded. "Personally, I think it should be Bethany. No offense, Allison, but she's a surgical nurse, and you're a pediatric nurse. Her skills are what Nikki needs if something goes wrong, not yours."

"No, I agree," Allison said, nodding. "It should be Bethany."

"Are you sure this isn't a way to keep me from seeing Thor again?" Bethany demanded.

Livvy shook her head. "No. If this works, you'll both come back to Alesia. We still have a shapeshifter to deal with, and Thor thinks he'll try to seize control of the portal again. Thor believes that Atreus is working for someone else who wants control of the portal, and that person will keep trying for as long as it takes."

Bethany nodded. "Good. I want Nikki to be okay, but I also want to have a long talk with Thor."

"Thor wants that, too. For now, he wants you and Nikki to stay here, and the rest of us to wait outside the building until you're through the temporary portal and are safely in Riverstone."

"I'll tell Peter and Kevin," Allison offered.

"And I'll tell Justin and Nikki," Livvy said.

Justin brushed the hair from Nikki's face. "I've missed you," he whispered.

"I missed you," she said softly.

Tears streamed down Justin's face. "I'm so sorry, Nichole. I promised you that I'd always have your back, but I failed. It's all my fault."

"No, it's not," Nikki told him. "They told me that you and the others were dead. I didn't want to believe them, but I knew that, if you were alive, you'd come for me, and I needed to survive until then. If you were dead, though, I knew I didn't want to be the sole survivor. I've been through that before, and I'll never go through it again. A life without you in it isn't one I want to live, so I refused to answer any of their questions. I wasn't going to give them the satisfaction of breaking me. All I wanted was to see you again, and that's one thing they couldn't give me. But I wasn't going to let them take anything else from me if they

The Portal of Alesia

were right and you were dead."

Tears welled up in Nikki's eyes, too, as a sharp pain tore through her body. "This is goodbye, isn't it?" she asked.

Justin nodded. Bethany had told him when she came to find him.

Nikki reached up and touched his face. "At least I got to see you one last time. I knew you'd find me and rescue me if you could. You kept that promise."

Justin couldn't say a word. He just stroked her face, trying to think of something to say.

Livvy and Bethany entered the room.

"Justin, you and I need to go outside. Nikki and Bethany are staying here."

Justin shook his head.

"Thor is going to create a temporary portal to send Nikki to Riverstone, and the tavern owner is going to send her back home. They're convinced that it will heal Nikki's wounds. Bethany is going with her in case something goes wrong. If it works, they'll both come back here so we can all finish the quest. But Thor needs us outside until Nikki and Bethany are safely in Riverstone."

Justin looked up at Livvy. He wiped the tears from his eyes. "This will cure her?"

"It should," Livvy said. "It did after the last quest, if you'll remember."

Justin nodded. He looked down at Nikki, who looked surprised by the news. He bent down and kissed her gently. "I'll see you soon, Nichole. I love you."

"I love you," Nikki said.

Justin stood, and he and Livvy left the building together.

Bethany knelt next to Nikki. "Are you ready for this?"

Nikki tried to shrug, but it didn't work too well. "Will it hurt?"

"I don't know. But if it cures you, what does it matter? What happens in a quest remains in that quest. We're about to put that to the ultimate test."

"And if it doesn't work?"

It was the measure of their friendship that Bethany said, "Then it was wonderful knowing you."

Nikki smiled.

Thunder sounded in the distance. Both Nikki and Bethany knew what that sound meant.

It sounded again, only louder. Bethany clutched Nikki's hand.

A bright flash like lightning filled the room and...

...They were in the tavern.

"Hang on," the tavern keeper said from behind the bar.

Another bright flash like lightning filled the tavern.

Nikki looked around her apartment. She was on her couch, and Bethany was sitting next to her. They were wearing the same clothes they had on before the quest began.

The tavern owner was on the TV screen. "I see you made it," he said. "Are you both okay?"

Bethany nodded. "I am."

She turned to look at Nikki, who stood up and walked over to the mirror just outside the kitchen. There were no cuts or bruises on her face. She lifted her shirt, and there were no bruises on her abdomen. Then she lifted the back

The Portal of Alesia

of her shirt and turned around. She couldn't see any whip marks anywhere.

Bethany stood and walked over to the mirror. She examined Nikki quickly. There were no indications of any injuries at all.

"How do you feel?" Bethany asked.

Nikki bent over, twisted around, and then said, "I feel great. It's like nothing ever happened."

"What a relief," the tavern owner said on the screen. "Thor was worried that it might not work, but it seems to have worked perfectly. Are you ready to come back and finish the quest?"

Bethany looked at Nikki. "You don't have to if you don't want to," she said. "No one will blame you. The portals healed your injuries, but you went through something terrible. If you want to tap out, just say so. I'll go back alone. Thor and I have some unfinished business anyway."

Nikki shook her head. "I'm not leaving Justin over there to fight without me. I'm going back, and we're all going to come back when the quest is over."

"Are you sure?" Bethany asked. "Are you *really* sure?"

"As sure as I can be," Nikki replied. She looked at the tavern owner on the screen. "Bring us back to Riverstone."

The thunder roared, and there was a flash of bright light that filled the apartment.

A moment later, Nikki and Bethany were back in the tavern. They were wearing the same clothes as when they had first arrived at the beginning of the quest. Nikki's armor shined, and her sword had no damage to the blade. It was as if they had never started the quest in the first place.

The tavern owner came around the bar and hugged them both.

"I'm so happy it worked and that you're able to come back and help the others finish this quest," he said. "I know Thor is waiting for you in Alesia, but if there's anything you want before I send you there, please ask."

Nikki shook her head, but Bethany looked pensive. "No," she finally said. "There's no reason to put this off any longer than necessary. You might as well send us through the portal."

The tavern owner nodded and returned to his place behind the bar. The familiar green oval appeared on the far wall, and a moment later, the portal opened. Bethany and Nikki could see Thor on the other side, waiting for them.

"Time to go," the tavern owner said.

Nikki and Bethany walked through the portal. A heartbeat later, they were standing next to the Portal of Alesia, and Thor was grinning from ear to ear.

"Welcome back!"

Chapter 9

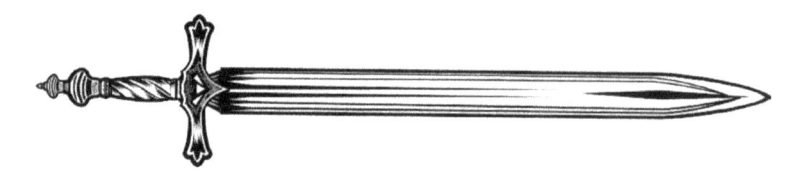

Nikki looked at Thor, then at Bethany, and then back to Thor. "I can't believe I'm back here so soon," she said, trying to break the uncomfortable silence. "Where are the others?"

"They're still at the barracks. I need to let them know you're okay and have them join us. In the meantime, shall we head up to the house? I have rooms prepared for you."

Thor led the way up the road to the Grand Master's residence.

"So how is it that you're the new Grand Master?" Nikki asked as they walked.

"I told Livvy, so the rest already know some of it," Thor answered. "Once everyone is together, I'll tell you the whole story. The long and short of it is that I was always supposed to be the next Grand Master. I learned that from the portal itself."

"And how does that work?" Nikki asked.

"Hard to explain, but every Grand Master except for

the very first one, has been from Earth and has found his way here just in time to step in as the new Grand Master. I'm just the latest one."

"So you would have been here to take over even if we hadn't already been here on a quest?" Nikki asked.

"As near as I understand what the portal told me... yes. The quest brought me here, but I would have been brought here regardless."

Bethany snorted but said nothing.

"Yes, I know we need to talk, Bethany," Thor said gently. "We will. I promise."

"I seem to remember another promise you made," Bethany snapped.

"And I haven't broken it," Thor reminded her. "It's just not going to be kept in the way we both imagined."

"What is that supposed to mean?" Bethany demanded.

"We'll discuss that in private."

They reached the residence a few minutes later.

"You've had a rough few days, Nikki," Thor said after he introduced her and Bethany to his assistants. "If you want to rest, I'll have someone show you to your room."

"Honestly, Thor, I feel great. Whatever happened to me back at the barracks went away as soon as the portal sent me home. Other than the memories, it's like nothing ever happened to me. I'm not sore, I'm not tired, I'm just a little confused about what's been happening lately."

"I'll bring you up to speed when the others arrive. That way everyone will hear it at the same time."

Nikki nodded. "I *am* hungry."

Thor smiled and gestured to one of his assistants. "Will you show Nikki to the kitchen and fix her whatever she wants?"

"Yes, Grand Master."

Nikki followed the assistant to the kitchen.

Bethany and Thor were alone in the entry hall. "If you'll give me a moment to send a message to Livvy, we can talk. Let's go into the library."

Bethany followed him to the library, the last place they were together before Thor was captured. Thor closed the doors behind them, moved the two oversized wingback chairs so they were facing each other close to the fireplace, and motioned for Bethany to sit down.

"Livvy, it's Thor." He reached out and spoke to Livvy's mind.

"Did it work?" Livvy asked.

"Perfectly. I want the rest of you to return here as soon as possible. We have information to share, and we have plans to make."

"I'll tell the others, and we'll be there in a few hours."

Thor sat across from Bethany. "I told Livvy that Nikki's fine and that the two of you made it back. They're on their way to join us."

Bethany nodded.

"Do you want to start, or do you want me to?" Thor asked.

Bethany didn't hesitate. In spite of the explanations and speculations that Livvy and Allison had shared with her, Bethany ripped into him with all the venom a ginger has at her disposal, letting her hurt and her sense of betrayal come pouring out. It was as if she had heard nothing that Livvy or Allison had said.

"And worst of all," she concluded, "you didn't say anything to me until the decision had already been made and carried out. How am I supposed to process that? I thought we were lovers. I thought we were planning a future together. But you made a fool out of me. Was it all a lie, or did you just see an opportunity and jump at it without any consideration for me?"

"Do you mind if I explain, or do you just want to yell at me some more," Thor asked.

Bethany glared at him and gestured for Thor to speak.

Thor took a deep breath and let it out slowly. "Okay. First of all, I never intended to become the new Grand Master. My plan was to help Boreas escape from Atreus and return here. Then I was going to contact the villagers and have them send over new assistants. I hoped that one of them could become the new Grand Master. This is before I discovered that the Grand Masters all came from Earth and were... destined, for lack of a better word, to become the new Grand Masters."

"Then why did you end up becoming the Grand Master?" Bethany demanded.

"I did it for you, and for the others. Boreas had been pressuring me to become his successor ever since he learned that the portal communicated with me when we first arrived here. But it wasn't until he reminded me that, if he died without a successor, the Portal of Alesia would shut down and never function again. That's when I realized I had no choice."

"I don't understand."

Thor reached out for Bethany's hand, but she pulled it away. "Look, Bethany, no one knows where Alesia is, apart from the Portal Keepers and possibly one or two others, and I have no idea how to get to Riverstone from here, even if Livvy transformed all of us into flying beasts. If the portal shut down, we'd have no way to get back to the tavern and

The Portal of Alesia

then home. We'd be trapped here in Alesia forever. I didn't want that for you and the others. You have lives to live, and I wanted you to live them, but the only way that could happen, the only way you'd ever be able to go home again, is if there was a new Portal Keeper for Alesia. Boreas was dying. I figured he had less than an hour left, and I was right. Plus, there was no one else that the portal would accept. I decided that I'd rather live here and let the rest of you go home, than to force all of us to remain here. One versus eight. In the end, there was only one decision."

Bethany thought about this for several minutes without saying anything. Everything that Livvy and Allison had said to her finally made sense, because she was ready to listen.

Once she realized why Thor had done what he had done, it touched her that he was willing to give up his entire life so she and the others could return home again. No one had ever sacrificed for her like that before, and as irritated as she was that his decision was made without her input, she understood that he really had no choice, other than to be selfish and force the entire team to never see home again. She felt the anger and betrayal drain from her as she realized just how far Thor would go to save her and the others, and it forced her to reexamine everything that she had been feeling since she had begun to suspect that Thor would be the new Grand Master.

Bethany's expression softened. Finally, she said, "So, you sacrificed yourself... for us?"

Thor nodded. "The hard part was walking away from my life on Earth, and potentially walking away from my life with you. The rest of it was easy."

"So want does this mean for us?" Bethany asked.

"I don't know. I really don't. I know that I love you, but I can't be selfish. I know how much your career means to you, how close you are to the promotion you've been working toward for years. I want to you get what you've earned. I want you to be able to live your life. You deserve that. Besides, what good is living here with me if it causes you to miss out on the job of your dreams?"

"Wait. You want me to stay here with you?" For some reason, that idea had never occurred to her before.

"Of course I do," Thor replied. "I had every intention of spending the rest of my life with you before all this happened. But I can't ask you to give up your career, your dreams, just to have you here with me. That's not right."

Bethany shook her head. "Thor, you're *part* of my dreams. What good is that promotion if you're not there to cheer me on? What good is a life if you're not a part of it?"

Thor leaned forward. "I don't know how to give you both. If you have me, you have to give up your career, your life, your friends. If you go back and get the job, you keep your career and your life and your friends, but you lose me. I can't tell you what to do, and I don't want you resenting me if you choose one and then regret it. Honestly, it might be better if you go home with the others. I'm easier to replace than everything you'd lose if you remained here."

Bethany shook her head. "Thor, you can't be replaced, and if I tried, I'd compare all men that I met to you, and they'd all come up short. I don't want to have to settle for one of them if there's a way I can still have you."

Thor nodded slowly. "You *can* have me, but not with the career you've devoted so much of your life to. All those years... would you really throw them away just to be with me? Could I live with myself if I let you do that?"

The Portal of Alesia

"That's not your choice," Bethany pointed out.

"No, it's *our* choice, but I won't put you in a position where you'd resent me because of all that you'd have to sacrifice just to be with me."

"But we'd be sacrificing for each other, Thor, and isn't that what people do when they're committed to a life together? You sacrificed for me. Could I say that we were truly in love if I didn't sacrifice for you? Otherwise, our relationship would never be one of equals. There would always be an imbalance, and that's what breeds resentment. It's not whether or not I had to give something up or you had to give something up, it's whether or not only *one* of us was willing to give something up that would eventually tear us apart." Bethany leaned back in her chair and stared at the wall over Thor's shoulder. "Okay. Let's look at this another way. What are the pros and cons of me staying and me going? What's the offer for me to stay here with you?"

It never occurred to Thor that she'd look at their relationship that way after only knowing each other for such a short time. He grinned. "A chance to live in paradise and explore the universe with me. A chance to help me with the more political aspects of my new responsibilities as the Grand Master of the Portal Keepers. And a chance to help the villagers and farmers here in Alesia with your medical skills, as limited as they'd be on this world. Plus, a chance for us to start a family together."

Bethany nodded. "That's a tempting offer. As for the cons, you've already listed them. Quitting my job, giving up my career, and giving up my friends. Like you, I have no family back home to leave. And if I return home with the others, I get to keep my job and my career, I'd get to keep my friends, but I'd lose you and the life we had planned together."

"Which you'd lose anyway, since most of our plans didn't take into account living on another world," Thor noted. "Yes, we'd be together, but not the way we had envisioned."

"Plans change," Bethany responded. "Whether we're here or back home, plans change when things happen. That's the nature of life. It's unexpected. I could get transferred to another hospital. You could get tenure at another school. Fifty miles away or an entire world away... the problem is the same. We'd have to readjust our plans to make the new reality work."

Thor cocked his head to one side. "Are you actually thinking about staying?"

Bethany shrugged. "Thinking, yes. Deciding... well... not yet. I still need to process everything for a while. And we still have the quest to complete, right?"

Thor nodded.

"So tell me about this destiny business you mentioned earlier."

Thor explained all that he learned from the portal when he bonded with it. Bethany listened to every word. Had anyone else told her what he just told her, she would have assumed that it was all garbage. But she believed Thor, and it helped her see that he truly didn't have a choice but to do what he did.

They talked for a while longer. Then Bethany asked, "So, where am I staying while I'm here?"

"I had a guestroom set aside for you," Thor answered, "in case you were too pissed to stay with me. But you're welcome to stay with me in my chambers."

The Portal of Alesia

Bethany smiled. "I'm suddenly very tired. Do you have plans for the next couple of hours?"

Thor understood. "None that are more important than being with you."

"Then why don't you show me to *our* chamber?"

Thor stood and held out his hand. "This way."

Atreus recognized the landscape below him. He was over the northern edge of the Realm of the High Kingdom. In the distance, he could see the palace, with its pennants flying in the breeze.

"Thank the heavens Telise's map was accurate," he thought as he dropped below the clouds. *"If it had been wrong, I'd still be flying over one of the oceans, and I'd probably drown."*

Part of him felt relief that he was back home, but he also dreaded his encounter with Princess Telise. Even though they had been lovers off and on, she was not someone to cross lightly. Many of her other lovers had disappeared over the years, and he didn't want to be the latest casualty of her wrath.

He circled the spires of the alabaster-colored stone palace, looking for a quiet place near Princess Telise's quarters to land and transform back into his human form. He found one and landed on the blue and gold polished stone tiles at the end of the corridor leading to her private apartment.

"What are you doing here, Atreus," a familiar voice behind him demanded.

Atreus felt a shudder go up his spine as he turned

around and faced her.

"Your Royal Highness! We have much to discuss. Is this a good time for you?"

Telise's expression was angry. "If you're here, that means you fucked up royally. Tell me why I shouldn't just kill you now."

"Because we can still achieve our goal. I have a plan to present to you. Will you at least hear it before deciding the time and means of my execution?"

Telise regarded him coldly, but there was a slight upturn on the edges of her tightly pursed lips. "You have audacity, Atreus. That's one of the things I always liked about you. Very well. Follow me so I can hear this plan of yours. I hope it's better than your last one."

"So do I," Atreus thought as he followed Telise toward her apartment. She wore a flowing sky-blue gown that accentuated her extraordinary figure. A simple gold circlet was all she wore in her long raven-colored hair to denote her rank as a Princess of the realm.

Two sentries opened the massive wooden doors to Telise's apartment—furnished in deep red fabrics—and closed them once she and Atreus had entered.

"What the hell happened?" Telise snapped when they were alone. "You should have come back through the portal as the new Grand Master. Instead you had to *fly* back here. Nice bird, by the way. I was watching it for quite a while, hoping that it wasn't you, since that bird isn't native to these parts. But it *was* you, so you'd better have a damn good explanation for why you're here and why I shouldn't remove your head from the rest of you."

"Your highness—" he began

"Oh, stop with the formalities, Atreus," Telise spat.

The Portal of Alesia

"We're alone."

Atreus bowed his head. "Very well, Telise. The Grand Master was closer to death than we knew. I thought he had weeks left. He only had days by the time we took him. He refused to make me his successor—kept going on and on about how the portal would never accept me, as if the portal were alive or something. Anyway, I had him isolated with only me there with him, so he'd have no choice but to choose me. He threatened to die without a successor and let the portal be shut down before he'd do that, but I was confident that I could change his mind."

"Which you obviously didn't," Telise observed. "So what happened? Did he die on you without a successor?"

Atreus shook his head. "No. The Keeper of the Portal of Riverstone hired eight people to find out what happened in Alesia and attempt to rescue the Grand Master. Two were sorcerers. The portal spoke to one of them."

"What?" Telise demanded. "What do you mean it spoke to him?"

"The portal actually communicated with him. He didn't understand what it said at first, but he did later. I sent men to abduct the sorcerer to keep him away from the portal and from me until after the Grand Master was dead. It never occurred to me that those idiots would imprison him right across the hall from the Grand Master. The sorcerer managed to escape from his cell and enter the Grand Master's cell. That must have been when the Grand Master made the sorcerer his successor."

Telise picked up a goblet and hurled it across the room. "A sorcerer as Grand Master? Can you imagine the protections he can put around the portal with that kind of power at his command? He could conquer the Eight

Realms with a wave of his hand." She shook her head. "Boy, when you fuck up, you really fuck up! And the Keeper of the Portal of Riverstone... That meddling busybody insists on interfering with my plans. Look at the mess he made in Cockaigne. All that work bribing, arming, and coaching Viscount Ladrach for nothing—all thanks to the group the Portal Keeper in Riverstone brought in to prevent the war I spent years trying to start. With Cockaigne tearing itself apart in a civil war, I could have sent the army of the High Kingdom in to restore peace, making that realm a protectorate of the High Kingdom. Viscount Ladrach would administer his realm on our behalf, and I could then use him to conquer the other realms until there was only one King or Queen in all of Annwyn."

"You?" Atreus asked.

"Of course, me!" she snapped.

"And your half-sister? She's the eldest of King Constantine's heirs. What about her?"

Telise smiled a wicked smile. "I have plans for her, just like I have plans for Riverstone. The first thing I need to do is to send more spies there to watch that Portal Keeper and see if the new Grand Master's companions or if the group that defeated Viscount Ladrach appear again. I want them punished for the *inconvenience* they've caused me."

"Where are you going to get more spies for Riverstone? Your current stable of spies is stretched somewhat thin at the moment, with all of the intrigue that you and the King are causing across the Eight Realms."

Telise thought about this. "Viscount Ladrach's soldiers are presently out of work, aren't they? Perhaps some of them would enjoy a change of scenery... and steady pay. I'll

The Portal of Alesia

send my spymaster to Cockaigne and see who might enjoy a different profession."

Atreus nodded.

"And their first job, after finding and capturing the people who've been interfered with my plans, is to find out where the Portal Keeper gets these people and why they're so good at shitting on everything I'm trying to accomplish. I need to know before the rest of my plans can be put in motion."

"There's more, Telise," Atreus said, returning to the subject of the new Grand Master. "The new Grand Master is also a shapeshifter. I was having the old Grand Master moved to get him away from the sorcerer's companions. The sorcerer was somehow hidden and went with the Grand Master. I guess the Grand Master died along the way. When I caught up to the wagon, it, the old Grand Master, and the three guards I sent with him had been incinerated with dragon fire. Since there are no dragons in Alesia, I assume the sorcerer changed shape to burn them and then assumed another shape to fly to the portal before I could catch up and stop him."

Telise drummed her fingers on the table next to her. "Any other fuck-ups you want to tell me about?"

"Yes, the men you sent with me were pathetic and stupid. I sent a squad to intercept and destroy the sorcerer's companions, and that squad was destroyed. One of the companions was a female warrior, and I had her captured for interrogation. The men I ordered to interrogate her decided to torture her instead, and they killed her. When her companions arrived at the barracks to rescue her, and they saw what had been done, it drove them in to a killing frenzy you've never seen before. They slaughtered all of the men who were still alive. A handful slaughtered twenty soldiers, and only one looked like he had died by a blade."

"What did they use?" Telise asked.

"Bare hands," Atreus replied. "Necks snapped, throats ripped, heads twisted off... it was the most gruesome sight I've ever seen. So much rage. I flew for the portal after that, just in time to see the sorcerer emerge from the portal as the new Grand Master. I dreaded having to return here and tell you of my failure, but I have another plan that I believe will work, and it fixes the flaw in the initial plan."

"Tell me, and let's see if it's good enough to spare your miserable life."

"First, where is your sister?"

"Angélique? She's on a campaign in an couple of the realms, dealing with problems that either I caused or the King allowed to happen and fester. Why?"

"Part of the plan. So, the flaw in the previous plan was that I didn't have any leverage over the old Grand Master to force him to name me his successor. He lived alone, except for his assistants, and they were all willing to die for him. The villagers and farmers in Alesia were also willing to die for him. There was no one that I could threaten that would force his hand. I don't think that's true with the new Grand Master."

"Explain."

"He arrived in Alesia with seven companions. Six are still alive. They've clearly known each other for some time. If I can take them, I have leverage that might force him to surrender his powers to me in exchange for their lives."

Telise nodded slowly. "Might force him... and what about the portal itself? Will it accept you even if you have the Grand Master's powers?"

"You don't believe that the old Grand Master was telling the truth about that, do you?" Atreus asked. "That's just nonsense. Portals aren't alive. Whoever has the power has control. End of story."

Telise's stare bore its way into his soul. "You'd better be right about this, Atreus. So, how do you plan to take the companions of this new Grand Master?"

"I need more soldiers than before. Proper troops, not those empty-headed thugs you gave me last time."

"You mean from the city garrison? Angélique's army? How am I supposed to get soldiers from the army to go to Alesia with you?"

Atreus smiled. "Because no one will know it's me. I'll transform myself into Angélique and order them to follow me. Then I'll tell *our* Portal Keeper that I'm going to pay homage to the new Grand Master and offer apologies for what happened with his predecessor. That should convince the fool to open the portal for me and the soldiers."

"And if the soldiers find out you're *not* Angélique?" Telise asked. "What do you think will happen then?"

"How could they possibly find out?" Atreus asked. *With that warrior girl dead, there's no one who can force me to return to my true form... other than perhaps the Grand Master. He is a sorcerer, after all.* He continued, "And even if they did, they'll have to follow my orders if they ever want to see home again. Otherwise, they'll be just as trapped, or just as dead, as I'll be."

Telise stared at Atreus, wondering what flaws were in this plan. It's not that Atreus was stupid, but he lacked the ability to see possibilities and plan for contingencies. If this plan didn't go exactly as expected, everything could fall apart quickly, and if the new Grand Master decided to retaliate against the realm of the High Kingdom, Telise's power, as well as her uncle's, could be lost forever. That was a disaster she couldn't risk.

"Let me think about it," she said finally. "Meanwhile, entertain me."

"How?"

She shot him an annoyed look.

"Oh, right. Strip."

She nodded.

Atreus complied. Telise stood, pushed him onto the wide chair she had been sitting on, and began stimulating him with her hands. When he was erect, she hiked up her dress, and mounted him, forcing him to penetrate her immediately. She rode him until he came inside of her.

She stood and held out her hand. "More."

He followed her to the second of her two bedrooms—the one decorated all in black and reserved for her sexual recreation. Soon, he was tied to the bed and gagged. Telise removed her dress and mounted him again.

Atreus admired the sight he had seen many times, but never tired of seeing. Her pert breasts, lean hips, toned butt and legs, flat stomach, and pale and unblemished skin enticed him every time, and this time was no different. Her breasts were erect and firm. He longed to hold them, but the bindings prevented that. He had no choice but to let her do whatever she wanted to do to him. This was for her pleasure after all, not his.

"Last longer, and you live longer," she whispered in his ear. "Cum that fast again, and you'll never leave this room alive."

Chapter 10

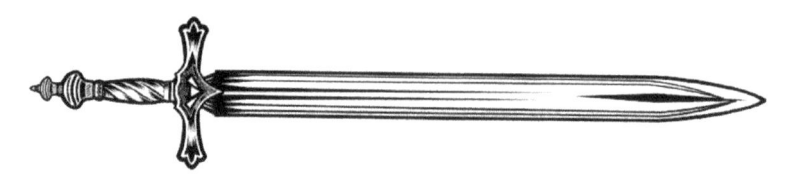

Nikki hadn't seen Thor or Bethany for several hours, and it made her smile. *Clearly, they've moved past whatever Thor did that made Bethany so angry.*

Her armor and weapons were in the chamber set aside for her and Justin. She had removed them hours earlier. She wore a leather doublet over her cotton shirt, which matched her leather trousers and boots. She had found it in the wardrobe cabinet in her chamber, and it fit her perfectly.

She sat by the fireplace in the library, legs crossed, enjoying the warmth and the smell of burning wood. A tankard of mead sat on the table next to her, and a crock of the best stew she had ever tasted sat on a plate next to that, along with a chunk of warm bread and butter.

"Do you need anything, ma'am?" one of Thor's assistants asked from the doorway.

Nikki looked at the young man and smiled. "No, thank

you. I have everything I need for now."

"Very well. I'll check back later."

The young man disappeared, leaving Nikki alone with her food... and her thoughts.

While she ate her stew and bread, Nikki thought about seeing Justin again. She was anxious for him to arrive with the others, not just because she missed him, but because he seemed so distant when they last saw each other. Nikki knew he felt responsible for what had happened to her, but it wasn't his fault. Now she had to convince him of this, or he might have a harder time recovering from what happened than Nikki would.

"I will not let him self-destruct because he thinks he failed me," she thought. *"He already avenged what happened to me, and that's enough. I'm okay, thanks to Bethany, Allison, Livvy, Thor, and the tavern owner. I don't need someone tiptoeing around me like I'm some fragile china doll. I need a lover. I need a fighter. I need a partner. Justin is supposed to be all that, and if he's going to fall apart from guilt and shame, then he's no good to anyone. He needs to move past this, just like I do, and now that I'm healed, it should be easier."*

She finished her food and sipped her mead, wondering when her friends would arrive.

Justin reached the top of the ridge and looked down at the valley below, bathed in moonlight from the full moon above. About four-hundred yards in front of him sat the Grand Master's residence.

"I'll let Thor know we're here," Livvy offered.

Justin nodded.

Livvy concentrated for a moment, and then said. "I told him."

"Let's go," Justin said. "It'll be good to be together again."

Livvy rode next to Justin. "Are you sure you're ready to see Nikki again without going all to pieces?" she asked.

Justin glared at her. "I'm not going to go all to pieces," he snapped. "She's okay. Everything's fine."

"Right," Livvy said sarcastically. "So all that moping and stoic behavior while she was unconscious, and the weeping right before Thor sent her back home, that was all just... what? Your reaction in the moment? Or was it unresolved feelings of guilt and shame because you think what happened to her is your fault? She doesn't blame you, you know, so why do you blame yourself? Are you sorry that she was hurt, or are you trying to destroy your relationship with her because things suddenly got too real for you? You forget, she was a soldier, and a damn good one, for almost ten years. She's a warrior. She knew the risks, and she faced them head-on. She was hurt, and now she's better. She survived. Avenging what happened to her... that balances the scales. You don't owe any more penitence for what Atreus and his men did to her."

Justin nodded, but he said nothing. Livvy touched a nerve that he had spent the entire ride from the barracks trying to resolve... to no avail. He knew that Nikki needed the man she fell in love with, not a man acting the way he had been acting for the last several days. But he had lingering doubts if he could be that man again. Only time would tell.

They rode down to the residence in silence.

Nikki heard someone coming down the stairs.

"Nikki?" It was Thor's voice.

Nikki looked toward the door. "In the library."

Thor appeared a moment later, followed by a flushed-but-happy Bethany. "They're here," he said.

Nikki jumped to her feet. Her face said everything; she was ecstatic to see everyone again.

The three of them exited the residence and stood at the edge of the courtyard as their friends arrived. Thor's assistants ran forward to take the reins of the horses.

Nikki couldn't wait a moment longer. She ran for Justin's horse and leaped into the air, catching him around his neck. He just barely managed to stay on his horse as Nikki hung on to him and kissed him.

The other questers just smiled and watched.

"I... missed... you," she said between kisses.

"I... missed... you, too," he replied.

He reached for her waist with both arms, swung a leg over the saddle, and slid to the ground with her.

The others dismounted and came forward to hug Nikki as Thor's assistants led the eight horses away to the stables.

"There's food waiting inside," Thor said. "Let's sit down, and then we can talk."

He led them into his new home. The men took their armor off and set it down in the hallway with their weapons. The ladies also disarmed. Then they all went into the kitchen to wash-up and eat dinner.

The kitchen table, large enough to seat twenty

The Portal of Alesia

comfortably, was already set for the guests. The exposed timber beams crisscrossed the room, and herbs and vegetables hung from wrought iron hooks spaced at even intervals. Most of the light came from the fireplace, but there were candles on the table and lanterns hanging from the beams.

The smell of the stew and bread woke everyone's appetites. Even Nikki, who had just eaten, took more.

Once they were seated, the team caught each other up on all that had happened over the previous week. Thor explained how he had become the new Portal Keeper and Grand Master. He included the choice he made to sacrifice himself for the others, but he played down the significance of that decision.

Kevin and Peter described how Justin dispatched the rest of Atreus' soldiers. Justin said nothing, but Nikki's expression said volumes. No one had told her exactly *how* Justin had avenged her, and even though she knew that he was a berserker, she was surprised.

"What did you do with all the bodies?" Nikki asked, never taking her eyes off Justin.

"I buried them in a mass grave away from the building," Livvy said. "It seemed disrespectful to leave that building with such a ghastly mess, given who originally built it. I removed all of the blood and gore, I also found and destroyed all of the tools and implements of torture that had been in the room where we found Nikki. Justin had thrown them into the brush outside, but I wanted them obliterated. I removed every hook, chain, and other fixtures in that room. No one will ever be hurt in there again, I promise you."

Thor explained how he got Nikki back home and then

brought her back to Alesia, and Nikki confirmed that she was completely healed and that there were no lingering effects from the torture, apart from the memory of what happened.

Bethany talked about the trip from the barracks to the tavern to home and back again. She also explained that she and Thor had talked, and she understood why he did what he did. She clearly had forgiven him, but she wouldn't comment on what his decision would do to their relationship.

Thor, seeing that everyone was too exhausted to talk strategy, said, "I had planned to discuss what happens next, but I think it might be best for everyone to get some rest first. We can discuss plans in the morning."

The assistants appeared and began cleaning the kitchen. They wouldn't let any of the questers assist, so everyone grabbed their belongings and headed to the chambers that Thor had set aside for them.

Peter and Allison wasted no time. As soon as they were inside their chamber with the door closed and locked behind them, they removed their clothes and crawled into the bed. Thor's assistants had already built a fire in each of the guest chambers, and there were pitchers of water, a basin, and towels in each of the rooms, so the questers could freshen up.

Allison pushed Peter onto his back and mounted him. She rubbed herself against him, stimulating him until he was fully erect. Then she guided him inside of her.

They made love several times that night, unable to feel

completely satisfied while they still had strength to continue. The fire had died down considerably before they finally decided that sleep was needed. They held each other close in the firelight and drifted off quickly.

Livvy and Kevin sat next to each other on the edge of the bed. Livvy was exhausted from having to protect everyone and from keeping Nikki alive until a way to get her home could be devised. The strain on herself had put a strain on her relationship with Kevin. He understood what she was going through and was determined not to add to it, but there were things they needed to discuss.

As tired as she was, Livvy wanted to discuss them before they went to bed.

"I know I haven't been myself lately," she said, "bossing everyone around, leading the team, all that. It's not me. You know that. It's just... with Thor gone, Nikki dying, and Justin... incapacitated, it all fell on me as the only sorcerer left. I never meant to ignore you or make it seem like I didn't value you. Circumstances got in the way of how I want to be around you, and I don't want you thinking that this is something you're going to see more of when we're together. Once this quest is over, and we're back home, things will be more normal, and we can continue building on what we started after the last quest."

She took his hands in hers. "Everything I want in this life is you, and I'll do anything to prove that to you every day that we're together." She looked at him. "That is what you still want, isn't it?"

Kevin smiled. "More than anything else in the world. I

understand what you've been going through. That's why I pulled back a bit. I didn't want to add to your burdens. You had enough to keep you busy without having to deal with relationship issues at the same time. The team needed you to step up, and you did. I admire that, even though I know it took a toll on you. Rest assured, I'm not going anywhere, and whether you're leading or I'm leading or no one is leading, there's nowhere else I want to be than at your side."

Livvy leaned forward and kissed him. It was the first kiss they had shared since the last time they were inside the residence, and it was electric.

After a few minutes, Kevin asked, "Do you mind if we discuss one more thing before we... you know...? There's something I've been meaning to mention since before the quest started, but I keep getting sidetracked. I don't want to wait a moment longer, okay?"

Livvy giggled. "Sure."

"As I remember, there's no news on the job search, right?"

"Right. Lots of interviews, no commitments."

"Well, you know that store adjacent to the Rock Climbing Center?"

"The one that used to be a diner?"

Kevin nodded. "It's coming available in the next week or so, and I was thinking about buying it. At first, I was planning to turn it into retail space, but given its size, we could turn it into retail space and a food service space. If I were to move forward with that, would you consider taking over the food service operations?"

"What kind of food options are you thinking about?" Livvy asked, excited.

The Portal of Alesia

"Whatever you want and whatever works best in the space," Kevin replied. "I know what I like to eat, but creating food is something else entirely. That's your expertise, and I would defer to you."

"So... what? We'd be partners in this?"

Kevin nodded. "Business partners and personal partners."

Livvy's eyes lit up. "I need to see the space, but I love the idea. Let's see if we can make it work!"

"The business... or the personal?" Kevin asked coyly.

Livvy pushed him back onto the bed and pulled her clothes off before joining him. "Both."

Nikki and Justin arrived at their chamber. The fire in the fireplace provided all the light necessary. Justin put his armor and weapons next to Nikki's. Then he stared at her in the firelight.

"It seems like weeks ago that we were in this chamber," Nikki said. "Then again, it seems like yesterday."

"Are all the wounds really healed?" Justin asked, walking toward her.

She removed the doublet and lifted her cotton shirt so he could see her back. "No trace, inside or outside. As soon as I arrived at my apartment, it was like nothing ever happened."

"I'm glad." Justin lifted off her shirt, walked around her—looking at all the places she had been injured—and then put his arms around her waist. "The shock of what happened... seeing you like that... It hit me harder than I thought it would... or could. I freaked out. I blamed myself, and even after I killed those responsible, I still felt terrible."

Nikki started to say something, but Justin stopped her. "What I'm trying to say is that I know I wasn't myself, and I wasn't being who and what you needed me to be. But I see things more clearly now. You're okay, and that's all that truly matters."

"And you're not still feeling guilty because of something that was never your fault?" Nikki asked.

Justin's eyes looked down. "Enough people have pointed out to me that I wasn't responsible for what happened to you, and they've also pointed out that avenging what happened to you balances the scales. I think they're right, although I wish there had been a way to keep you safe. I was hit from behind, and I didn't regain consciousness until well after you had been taken. I'm not sure what I could have done to prevent that."

"Nothing. And I don't blame you for anything that happened. You found me and rescued me, you avenged me, and you kept me safe until Thor and the tavern owner could work out a plan that the rest of us could never have devised. All in all, I feel lucky, and I feel loved. You're the love of my life, and as long as I have your love, I know I'm safe. Knowing that you loved me is what gave me the strength to endure what happened, so in a way, you *did* save me and keep me safe."

Justin pulled off his shirt. Then he held her close, feeling skin on skin for the first time in several days. He ran his fingers gently through her hair. "I can't promise that I'll always keep you safe from harm, but I promise that I'll never stop trying."

"Me, too," Nikki whispered. "And since that's the best

The Portal of Alesia

we can do, that's all we can expect of each other: to just keep trying and to keep loving each other."

"I do love you, Nichole."

"And I love you, too."

Nikki pulled his head down so she could kiss him. Then she finished undressing him while he undressed her. As they embraced again, Nikki whispered, "You'd better be rested, because I have all of my strength back, and sleep is gonna have to wait."

She started pushing him back toward the bed, and then she added, "And as for that thing you did to me last time, let's see if we can stay dryer tonight. There are too many ears in this building who don't need to hear you do that to me again."

Justin flashed a wicked grin. "I'll see what I can do about tonight, but don't think it won't happen again... and again... and again at some point in the future."

Nikki giggled.

They hurriedly washed each other. They normally liked to take their time, using the washing as part of foreplay, but they both needed to be connected, and it just wouldn't wait.

Nikki pushed Justin onto his back and climbed on top, so they could orally stimulate each other at the same time. Nikki teased Justin, getting him erect and stimulated, but not letting him finish. Then she lay next to him and pulled him on top. He penetrated her immediately and began thrusting. Nikki orgasmed almost immediately, and Justin climaxed soon after.

Justin didn't stop, and Nikki wrapped her legs around him and kept her arms around his shoulders. She wanted him to continue, and he obliged.

After Justin came the second time, they rolled over so Nikki was on top. She pinned his arms above his head as she raised and lowered her pelvis while kissing him, increasing speed as she felt him getting close to cumming for the third time. She had lost count of her own orgasms, and she didn't care. They weren't keeping score, they were trying to share as much pleasure as they could stand.

When she felt him release, she lay on his chest, trying to catch her breath. The next thing she knew, Justin had pushed her off and was washing between her legs. Once he had finished drying her, his head moved between her legs, and his tongue began stimulating her. She had several more orgasms, because he wouldn't stop.

When he finally slowed down so she could relax, he used his hands to spread the lips between her legs. Then he blew, forcing his breath to strike her clit.

One of the most powerful orgasms she had ever had—not counting when she squirted the last time they were together—hit her and caused her to spasm uncontrollably.

"What did you do?" she whispered once it subsided.

"What... you mean this?" He did it again, with the same result.

"You're not touching me! How are you doing that?"

Justin explained. Before he could do it to her again, she moved her hand down and covered her clit. "I can't take anymore," she whispered. "I can't."

Justin moved up next to her. "Okay. I guess that's enough for one night. We'll have to do it again sometime."

"Sometime soon," Nikki said, snuggling close to him.

"I think I can accommodate that," he whispered in her ear. "I love you, Nichole."

"I love you."

Chapter 11

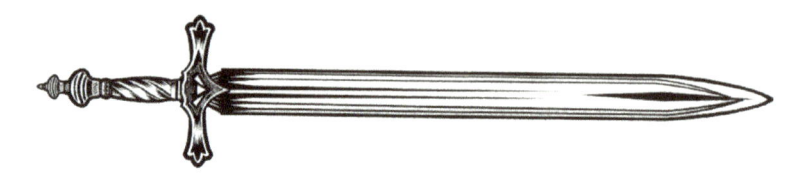

The questers met for breakfast the next morning, feeling rested, satisfied, and happy that a number of issues had been resolved in the night. They sat at the table together, along with Thor's assistants. He wanted everyone to help plan for whatever Atreus might do next to force Thor to surrender control of the portal.

"So what went wrong with Atreus' first plan, Grand Master," asked one of Thor's assistants named Milos.

"We did," Livvy answered. "I don't think he was prepared for anyone to interfere with his plans, nor do I think he ever imagined that one member of our company would become the new Grand Master."

"He certainly never imagined that we'd have two sorcerers on the team," Thor added. "That had to really throw off his plans. So... what else went wrong?"

"What his men did to Nikki," Kevin said. "It put Justin in such a rage that he wiped out the rest of Atreus' men."

Thor nodded. Nikki looked over at Justin and smiled

at him. Justin winked at her, but said nothing.

"He also didn't understand how portals pass from Keeper to Keeper," Thor said. "He was convinced that Boreas could name his successor, that that was all that was necessary. He never understood that the portal must approve of the selection, or the successor will never be able to control the portal. That was perhaps his most fatal flaw."

"So he thought that, if he could keep Boreas isolated, Atreus would be selected as the successor by default?" Milos asked.

Thor nodded. "And nothing would convince him otherwise."

"Did Atreus give Boreas a reason to name him as his successor?" Peter asked. "What I mean is, did he have any kind of leverage over Boreas to force his hand, or was Atreus assuming that Boreas' approaching death would convince him to name anyone nearby as his successor so the portal would have a Keeper?"

"I don't know," Thor conceded, "but you bring up an interesting question."

"Atreus could never use the villagers or farmers in the area to force Boreas to submit," Milos said. "Boreas knew that we'd all gladly lay down our lives to protect him and the portal. That wouldn't have worked."

"And Boreas had no family," Thor informed them.

"So Atreus had no leverage," Peter concluded.

"It seems not," Livvy said. "But that might not be true of Thor."

Thor looked very uncomfortable.

"What do you mean?" Kevin asked, watching Thor's reaction.

"Us," Nikki said. "If Atreus knows that we arrived with

The Portal of Alesia

Thor, then he might assume we could be used as leverage—especially Bethany."

"Would he be right, Thor?" Livvy asked.

Thor didn't answer right away. Then he said, "No. He's not right. I'm sorry, but my first duty is to the portal. Protecting it is my primary responsibility, and I have to be willing to sacrifice any and everything to keep it safe. If Atreus captured you, I'd try to rescue you, but I could not let him use you to force my hand and surrender the portal. The portal wouldn't let me, even if I wanted to."

"But Atreus doesn't know that, does he?" Milos asked.

"So?" Livvy asked, shocked by Thor's answer.

Milos explained. "If he thought that isolating Boreas would force Boreas to surrender his powers, Atreus probably thinks that capturing all of you would force the Grand Master to do the same. He doesn't know the Grand Master or the demands placed on him by the portal. Atreus could still try to capture all of you, hoping that it would work. Expecting it to work, only realizing too late that it was a waste of time."

"You make a valid point, Milos," Thor said. "The question isn't what Atreus might do that would work, it's what Atreus might do that he *thinks* would work, and taking all of you hostage to use as leverage over me is the kind of plan he might make."

"Would you really sacrifice us to save the portal?" Livvy asked, unable to get past this revelation.

Thor stared at her. "First of all, you have the power to transform everyone on the team into another shape so you can escape. You're a shapeshifter and a sorcerer, so you could do substantial damage to Atreus and his men. Plus you have three of the finest warriors I've ever seen as your companions. You'd be able to handle Atreus and his men long before he could use you against me. But should all of that fail, and he does use you against me, I'd never be able to accept his terms for your release. I cannot surrender the portal to him. It is not possible. I'm sorry, but it's not. But, as I said, I'm not worried. You all have more than enough skills to get out of any situation that he creates."

Livvy turned to Bethany. "Did you know about this?"

Bethany nodded. "Thor explained it to me yesterday. I didn't really understand it, because I still don't fully grasp the relationship between the Keeper and the portal, but I knew that he'd never be able to surrender the portal or his powers to another unless that person was accepted by the portal first. Boreas would never have been able to surrender the portal and his powers to Thor if Thor hadn't already been accepted by the portal."

Livvy sat back in her chair and crossed her arms. "Wow," is all she said.

"So how does this help us?" Kevin asked.

"I think we have to proceed as if Atreus will attempt to capture the rest of us and use us to force Thor to submit," Peter said. "We need to set up a watch for Atreus and his men, we need to monitor anyone coming through the portal, and we need to know what we'll do if we're captured so we can thwart Atreus' plans before he can present his terms to Thor."

"That's a good plan," Justin said, speaking for the first time. "If we already have a strategy in place, in case we're captured, then we'll know what to do without hesitation or further discussion, which should catch Atreus and his men off guard."

They spent the next hour discussing alternatives that

The Portal of Alesia

could be used if the questers were captured. When they felt they had a workable plan, Thor adjourned the meeting.

Milos and the other assistants began cleaning the kitchen. As everyone else left, Livvy pulled Bethany aside.

"So what's going to happen when this is over? Are you going back with us, or are you staying here with Thor?"

"We're still discussing that," Bethany said. "Whichever path I chose has pros and cons. I just have to decide what I can live with and what I can't."

"You'd give up your career? Your friends? Us?"

"That's part of what I'm wrestling with," Bethany replied. "The short answer is, I don't know. Not yet."

Livvy let go of Bethany's arm. "I can't imagine not having you around," Livvy said.

"I can't either, but I also can't imagine not being with Thor, and he's staying here when the rest of you leave."

"When will you decide?"

"I have until we return to Riverstone. After that, it'll be too late, one way or the other."

Princess Telise unstrapped the restraints keeping Atreus from moving. Then she removed the gag that kept him quiet.

"Good Morning," she said as the light from the sunrise bathed her naked body in golden light.

"Morning," Atreus mumbled, rubbing his wrists to restart the circulation and moving his jaw around to work out the kinks from being gagged all night.

"Ah, don't be like that," Telise purred. "You lasted much longer each time we did it. That earned you a stay of execution. You should be happy about that."

"A stay of execution? For how long?" Atreus asked.

"As long as I feel like," Telise responded. "Now show me some gratitude."

She reached down and grabbed him. He didn't think he could manage another erection for at least a week, but it responded to her touch immediately. She moved her hand up and down, stimulating him to make the erection even harder.

Once he was fully erect, he pushed her to her knees and penetrated her from behind. He grabbed her hips, holding onto them as he thrust. Deeper and deeper he thrust, and she squealed with delight as he hit the sensitive spot that could only be reached from that position.

As he thrust, he let go of one of her hips and moved his thumb to stimulate her other hole. Then he inserted his thumb as he thrust. She shuddered. Then she reached around and pulled him out.

"Move your thumb out of the way," she commanded, breathlessly.

He complied and penetrated the other hole where his thumb had been. Her back arched as he went deeper and deeper. Suddenly, her knees gave way, and she fell flat onto the bed, sprawled with her arms and legs forming a four-pointed star. Atreus maintained the connection and continued thrusting.

Telise's face was buried in the sheets, muffling her moans and screams. She reached down with one of her hands so she could stimulate her clit as his thrusting became more intense.

Her first orgasm caused her to tremble, but the second one left her shaking as she spasmed from the double

The Portal of Alesia

stimulation.

Atreus did everything he could think of to make it last as long as possible, but he reached a point where his release couldn't be stopped. He came inside of her and then lay against her back, panting from the workout.

Telise laughed. "My, my, my... what brought that on? It's not like you to try something different."

"If this was the last time, I wanted it memorable," Atreus said, nibbling on her earlobe.

"It was certainly that," Telise confirmed. "And it earned you a reprieve. Now, get off me and tell me your plan again. I'm ready to listen, this time."

Atreus rolled off the Princess and lay next to her. He told her his plan again, and she listened carefully to every bit of it.

"So you're going to impersonate my sister, take the soldiers through the portal, capture the Grand Master's companions, and hold them hostage until he surrenders the portal to you?"

Atreus nodded. "And I'll hang one hostage a day until he complies. In fact, I'll hang them from the branches of a tree that faces his residence on the opposite ridge. Their rotting bodies will remind him of what's at stake."

"And no one will be able to see through your disguise?" she asked.

Atreus shook his head, confident that, with the warrior girl dead, no one else had the power to force him back into his true form.

Telise nodded. "I think that's a much better plan than the last one. Leverage is always a better inducement than simple logic. My uncle taught me that. Fortunately, the new Grand Master has something you can leverage."

She looked at him and added, "Have you thought about what you'll do if you end up killing all of the hostages and the Grand Master still won't give in?"

Atreus shrugged. "My first inclination was to torture him, but he's a sorcerer and a shapeshifter. That would be pointless. He could escape from any confinement I created for him. He's already proven that. He maintains a shield wall around the residence and the portal, so I couldn't attempt to assassinate him or wound him severely enough that he'd have to transfer his powers to someone quickly. The villagers and farmers in the area would all gladly die for him, so they can't be threatened. It's much more likely that, should I end up killing all of his companions without convincing him to surrender the portal to me, he'll come after me and the soldiers, and with his powers, I doubt any of us would survive. He's already proven that he enjoys using dragon fire, and he could incinerate all of us in under a minute if he put his mind to it."

"So... you'll either succeed or die?" Telise asked.

Atreus nodded. "I don't see a third option, but if you do, I'm happy to listen."

Telise shook her head. "I thought about it all night, but I don't see one either. This is no ordinary foe you're going up against. Short of a dragon-versus-dragon fight, I don't see how you'd best him, and even if you defeated him, there's no guarantee that he'd ever surrender the portal to you. It all comes down to his companions and what he'll be willing to do to save them from death."

"There's something else to consider," Atreus said. "If the Grand Master defeats me and the soldiers, and he discovers that I was impersonating your sister to get the soldiers through our portal to Alesia, you can bet that

The Portal of Alesia

Essien won't be Keeper of the Portal of the High Kingdom much longer. That's another ally that you'd lose from this business."

Telise tugged at her lower lip. "I have a back-up plan if that happens," she said. "Remember, this is just one part of a much larger plan."

"Ending with you becoming the High Queen?" Atreus asked.

Telise smiled. "Of course."

"That's a lot of people who have to die to make that happen... here and in the other realms. Are you really prepared to cause that much death and destruction just to be High Queen? And are you prepared to hold the realms under your rule once you wear the crown? I know your temperament and your tastes, and they might spark an uprising that would end the realms for generations to come, with your head being displayed on a pike in front of the ruins of this palace."

Telise slapped him across the face so hard that her handprint remained on his face as a red welt.

"You forget yourself, Atreus," she spat. "Just because we fuck doesn't give you the right to question or accuse me. What you just said could be considered treason."

"If you were High Queen, it would be treason, Telise," Atreus said evenly. "But you're a Princess who can only become High Queen upon the deaths of your uncle and your sister, and contemplating what you're contemplating is treason on *your* part. I don't care one way or the other, but I don't want you to put a plan in motion if it could backfire and end in your execution. If you move forward, I want you to succeed. That's not treason, that's loyalty, and I'll always be loyal to you. Always."

Telise clenched and unclenched her fist, as if debating whether she wanted to strike him again. Eventually, her hand dropped. "You're right. I need to make certain that none of my plans backfire, and that includes your plan to seize the Portal of Alesia. For that reason, if it looks like your plan will fail, you cannot allow yourself to be captured. You must escape, or you must sacrifice yourself to keep our secrets secret. Do you understand?"

Atreus nodded. "I knew already that I'd never return here once I left for Alesia. I'll either become the Portal Keeper and the Grand Master, or I'll be dead. But I'll make certain that your secrets are safe no matter what happens."

Telise leaned forward and kissed the cheek that she had slapped. Her handprint was still visible on his skin, and he winced when her lips touched it.

"Does it still hurt?" she asked, gently.

"No more than the other times you've hit me," he replied.

"Well, that was the last time I'll ever strike you." She patted her butt and added, "Just like this was the last time you'll ever do that to me."

Atreus smiled. "Then I hope it was as memorable for you as it was for me."

Telise smiled, but said nothing.

Atreus strode into the barracks of the city garrison soldiers who were deployed around the High Kingdom when the rest of the army was on campaign in the other realms. He had transformed himself into the likeness of Princess Angélique, commanding general of the armies of the High

The Portal of Alesia

Kingdom, who was a tall, muscular, and beautiful auburn-haired woman and fierce warrior. Her soldiers were surprised to see her.

"General! What are you doing here?" the colonel commanding the city garrison soldiers asked when she walked into his office.

Atreus looked disgusted. "This business with the new Grand Master," he replied with Angélique's voice. "The king and my sister made a mess of things between the High Kingdom and the previous Grand Master, and now I need to step in and smooth things over so we don't lose our portal or our portal privileges."

"What can I do to help?" the colonel asked.

"I need an honor guard of fifty of your best soldiers to accompany me to Alesia to see what can be done to salvage things with the new Grand Master."

"Why so many? If you don't mind my asking," the colonel inquired.

"There are six troublemakers who have taken refuge in Alesia. While I'm negotiating with the new Grand Master, I need the soldiers to track down these troublemakers and capture them. I may have to use them as part of my negotiations."

The colonel nodded, understanding the value of hostages during a negotiation. "When do you need the men ready?" he asked.

"Tonight," Atreus answered. "I want our arrival in Alesia to be unseen, so we'll arrive at night and head for a place where the men can make camp. Then we'll find the troublemakers before I present myself to the new Grand Master."

"Yes, General. The men will be ready."

"Good, Colonel. I'll be here at nine o'clock to give them final instructions and lead them to the portal."

"Yes, General."

Atreus left the barracks and headed for the Portal Keeper's residence. He still needed to convince Essien to open the High Kingdom's portal and allow him and the soldiers through to Alesia.

Essien saw Atreus approaching, and, thinking that it was Angélique, he raced outside to greet her.

"Princess Angélique, to what do I owe this pleasure?"

Atreus used the same story he had given the colonel, about having been recalled from her campaign in the other realms to repair the mess that her sister and uncle had made by sending Atreus to Alesia to influence the change of Grand Master.

"I completely understand," Essien said. "I've met the new Grand Master, and he is quite put out with the High Kingdom at the moment. Anything that heals that breach would be in all of our best interests. If he should decide to close our portal, the High Kingdom would cease to be the High Kingdom any longer, and that would be a tragedy."

"You see things perfectly, Essien," Atreus said. "That's why I'm taking an honor guard with me as a sign of respect. Do you think you could open the portal for us tonight? I want to present myself at first light and see if we can get things on track as quickly as possible. I need to get back to the army as soon as possible, so the faster I can conclude business with the new Grand Master, the better for us all."

Essien nodded. "It would be my honor, Princess Angélique. What time will you need the portal opened?"

"Ten o'clock this evening."

"All will be ready for you," Essien promised.

"Thank you." Atreus turned and headed back to Telise's apartment. When he arrived, he transformed back into his real form.

"How did it go?" Telise asked when he entered her apartment.

"Everything's ready. We leave tonight."

Atreus, disguised in the form of Princess Angélique, met the soldiers at the city garrison barracks at nine that night. After a quick inspection, Atreus and the soldiers mounted their horses, and he led the men to the portal.

Halfway there, he stopped and addressed the men, making sure no one else could hear what was being said.

"Men, it is true that we're going to Alesia. I have business with the new Grand Master. But my business is not what you were told. I'm not going to apologize for the High King's actions concerning the previous Grand Master. I'm going to dictate terms to the new Grand Master. No longer will the High Kingdom be at the mercy of the Brotherhood of Portal Keepers. It is my intent to add Alesia and Riverstone to the High Kingdom's domain. *That* is why we're going to Alesia.

"The new Grand Master has six companions that we're going to use as leverage over him. Our first mission will be their capture. Then I'll begin the negotiations, using them as a key part. As the High King has taught us, it is better to negotiate from strength, and that is what I intend to do. That is why I have chosen you to accompany me. No one must know of our real mission. Do you understand?"

The soldiers affirmed that they understood.

"Good. You will have to lead your horses through the portal. Once on the other side, mount up and ride east. I will lead you to the barracks that I've prepared for us to use. We have to ride right below the Grand Master's residence, and it is vital that no one in the residence know that we have arrived or where we've gone. So be swift, and be silent."

Atreus turned and led them to the Portal.

When they arrived, they dismounted. Essien opened the portal, and Atreus led the men and their horses through the portal.

Once on the other side, Atreus and the men mounted their horses and rode up the valley between the two ridges, being as quiet as possible. Once all of the soldiers were through the portal, it closed behind them.

Atreus glanced up at the Grand Master's residence, and he didn't see any light coming from the windows. He smiled, thinking that his plan was working and that no one knew he had returned to Alesia.

None of the soldiers noticed the two barn owls perched on one of the branches that the soldiers rode underneath. Once the soldiers had all passed, the owls took to the air and followed the soldiers east.

Chapter 12

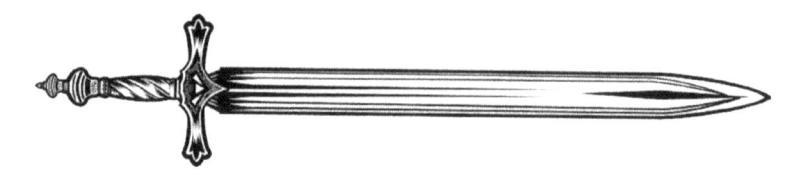

Livvy and Kevin, in the form of barn owls, flew after the soldiers who had come through the portal. They had been performing aerial reconnaissance ever since the team had developed a plan to deal with Atreus and Princess Telise, should there be an attempt to seize the portal again. Livvy had chosen the form of owls for night reconnaissance because they could fly almost silently and had great night vision.

"Did you recognize who was leading the soldiers?" Kevin asked.

"Not in that form," Livvy replied. "Looked like a woman, didn't it? It wasn't. It was Atreus disguised as Princess Angélique. His mind is an easy one to read. Their plan is to kidnap us and leverage us against Thor. Atreus plans to execute us one a day until Thor gives in."

"And he brought fifty soldiers with him to make it happen?" Kevin asked.

"Yes, but the soldiers don't know that they've been

deceived. They don't know their leader isn't Princess Angélique. If they did know, I doubt they'd follow orders any longer."

"Then our plan will work?"

"It should," Livvy communicated. "We'll make ourselves easy to capture, and once we've been taken to their camp, we'll throw a few surprises their way."

"Do you think Nikki is ready for this?"

"I think she was born for this," Livvy replied. "I can't wait to see the look on Atreus' face."

Livvy and Kevin followed the soldiers in the moonlight to the building Atreus had used as a barracks once before. They waited until the soldiers were assigned quarters, the horses had been stabled, and guards had been posted. Then they flew back to the Grand Master's residence.

Livvy and Kevin landed on the roof of the residence and changed back into their natural form. They walked downstairs, where Thor and the rest of their companions were waiting.

Nikki was lounging on one of the wingback chairs, with her legs draped over the armrest. Justin was sitting on the floor underneath her legs, and the rest of the couples were sitting together around the room. Thor was at his desk, and Bethany was sitting on the desk, facing him.

"We heard the horses and knew that someone had come through the portal," Nikki said.

"And I knew that someone had activated the portal," Thor added. "That's something that Essien doesn't know about. My portal tells me whenever anyone tries to use it."

"So what did you see?" Nikki asked.

"Fifty soldiers from the High Kingdom, led by Princess Angélique herself," Livvy replied. "Only it wasn't Princess Angélique, it was Atreus using her form. The soldiers have no idea that Atreus is leading them."

"And what is Atreus' plan?" Justin asked.

"As we suspected," Kevin answered. "Kidnap us and use us as leverage to force Thor to surrender the portal to him. He plans to kill one of us a day until you comply."

"So we follow the plan?" Nikki asked. Her eyes lit up with excitement.

Livvy nodded. "We let ourselves be captured, and then, once we've been taken to the ancient building they're using as their barracks, we turn the tables on him."

Looking at Nikki, Livvy added, "Nikki, they're using the same building where you were... where they..."

"Where I was tortured?" Nikki finished. "It's okay, Livvy. I'm not gonna go all to pieces seeing that building again. I'll be disguised, so Atreus won't recognize me or have a reason to single me out for... special treatment. And then, when I reveal myself, or when I reveal the form you've changed me into, I'll be having too much fun at his expense to let what happened to me enter into things. Relax. It's all going to go as planned. I'll be fine."

"And we'll all be there to make sure of that," Justin added, reaching up and putting a hand on her leg.

Nikki patted his hand.

"You should all get some sleep," Thor suggested, standing. "You'll need to be rested for this to look believable. We want all of you captured together. Less chance of someone getting injured that way. And remember... If the soldiers don't do what we expect them to do, Livvy will transform you into dragons, and you'll incinerate all of them on the spot. Don't take any risks, and no hand-to-hand combat. You're no match for fifty armored soldiers, berserker or not."

Thor looked directly at Justin, who nodded in agreement.

"All right," Thor said, taking Bethany by the hand. "See you all at breakfast."

As Thor and Bethany climbed the stairs to Thor's chamber, he asked, "Are you still sure you want to be with the others when they're captured?"

"Yes," she answered. "If something goes wrong, they'll need me. And if the soldiers are expecting a certain number of companions, they need to see all of us for this to work."

Thor nodded. "I'm worried," he said. "I'm worried Atreus might find out about us. That's leverage that would be too good for him to pass up, which puts you in extra danger."

They entered Thor's chamber, and he closed the door behind them. "I know, Thor, and I appreciate the concern. But as you've pointed out before, between Livvy and the others, nothing should happen to any of us. We should be able to spring our trap quickly and end this before things get out of hand."

"It is a good plan," Thor conceded. "Nikki's the key. If everyone can keep her safe—physically and emotionally—everything should go perfectly."

"Exactly," Bethany stated. She put her arms around

The Portal of Alesia

his neck. "Now take me to bed before I decide I'm too tired for what I want to do right now."

Thor grinned. "We wouldn't want that, would we?"

The next morning, the companions met for breakfast just after dawn.

"Forty soldiers are moving into position—half on the ridge above us, and half down in the valley. The other ten are remaining at the barracks." Livvy said. She and Kevin had taken the form of owls again and flown around the area to see where the soldiers were.

"Then we'll let them capture us this morning," Justin said. "Is everyone ready?"

"I will be," Nikki said. Looking at Livvy, she asked, "Are you sure my voice will be right?"

Livvy nodded. "The transformation will be complete, including the voice. And you already know how to wield a sword. Just stay beneath your traveling cloak until it's time to reveal yourself."

They ate quickly, and then they finished dressing and arming themselves. Thor's assistants saddled the horses and made sure the saddlebags were filled with food and any other supplies they needed.

As the sun shined brilliantly down the valley toward the portal, the companions mounted their horses and rode east, as if they were exploring the area.

Once they reached the top of the ridge and were out of sight of the residence, they found their path blocked by twenty soldiers.

"What is your business here?" Justin demanded.

"Soldiers of the High Kingdom are forbidden from entering Alesia—especially armed. I suggest you leave before the Grand Master becomes aware of your presence here."

The captain commanding the soldiers smiled. "My name is Captain Edmond, and the High Kingdom doesn't answer to anyone, good sir, nor does its soldiers recognize any authority apart from our general and our King. Our general has business with the Grand Master and doesn't wish to be disturbed. Come with us, quietly, allowing her to conclude her business, and we can all be on our way."

"And if we refuse?" Justin inquired.

"Twenty to seven is not promising odds," the captain said. The other squad of soldiers arrived from the valley below and joined Captain Edmond's men. "And forty to seven is even worse. There's no need for you to die here today. Come with us, and you'll be well treated."

Justin looked at his companions, and he winked at Nikki. Then he turned to the captain. "Very well. On your word that we'll be treated well, we'll go with you."

Justin reached for his sword to hand it to the captain, but the captain held up his hand. "No need for that. There are more than enough of us to deal with any deceit on your part. We'll disarm you when we reach our barracks."

Justin removed his hand from his sword. "Lead on, Captain."

Twenty soldiers took the lead, and twenty moved behind the companions. They rode east, toward the building where Nikki had been tortured.

Nikki kept the cowl of her traveling cloak pulled down over her face, so none of the soldiers would see the auburn hair or the form Livvy had transformed her into.

Atreus, in the form of Princess Angélique, approached the Grand Master's residence and stood just outside the shield wall that protected the building.

"I wish to speak to you, Grand Master," he shouted.

Thor stepped out of the residence and stood on the front porch. "Princess Angélique? Back again so soon? I thought we had concluded our business already."

"What are you talking about?" Atreus demanded.

"What do you mean? You came here at dawn, we talked, and you left. Now you're back. Is there something we didn't discuss earlier, or have you had a change of heart about what we agreed to?"

Atreus was confused, but he was also frightened. If Princess Angélique had come to Alesia to meet with the Grand Master, then he was in deep shit.

Thor stared at Atreus, and then he smiled. "Ah, I see it now. You're not the real Princess Angélique, are you... Atreus-the-shapeshifter? And you didn't know she was here in Alesia, did you? We'll, your soldiers probably know by now, or they will shortly. You may want to reconsider your plans."

Thor turned and headed back into the residence. When he reached the open front door, he looked over his shoulder and added, "Is there anything else we need to discuss? Your plan to leverage the hostages you took against me? Your plan to execute them one a day until I surrender the portal to you? Yes, I know your plans, Atreus. I suggest you worry about saving your neck and forget about your foolish plans."

With that, Thor entered the residence and shut the

door behind him.

Atreus was in a state of panic. He mounted his horse and raced east after the soldiers and their captives.

"I need the soldiers to find the Princess and take her captive. I can't use her as leverage against the Grand Master, but I can keep her from giving orders to the soldiers, and I can remove one of the two obstacles from Telise's desire to become High Queen."

The soldiers and their captives arrived at the barracks before noon. Once everyone dismounted, the companions made a great show of disarming themselves. They removed swords and daggers from their clothing, and more weapons from their saddles.

They created so much confusion, between removing the weapons and surrendering them to the soldiers, that no one noticed Nikki slip through the soldiers.

Nikki felt nothing as she looked at the barracks, but she turned her back to it anyway.

After she had stepped around the soldiers, she removed her traveling cloak. What no one had noticed is that Livvy had transformed Nikki into the likeness of Princess Angélique. She had gotten a good look at the form Atreus had taken the night before, and she had made Nikki look exactly the same. The long auburn hair looked like burnished copper in the sunlight.

Nikki turned and faced the soldiers, who were in a general state of disarray, thanks to her companions.

"What is the meaning of this nonsense?" she demanded at the top of her voice, her tone as fiery as her

The Portal of Alesia

hair. "Captain Edmond, are you completely incapable of controlling your men?"

The soldiers froze when they heard her voice, and they all turned and immediately came to attention when they saw Nikki.

Captain Edmond ran forward and stopped in front of her. He saluted.

Nikki acknowledged the salute and said, "How hard is it to disarm six captives, Captain?"

"I'm sorry, General," the captain said. "It'll be completed immediately."

He turned to issue orders, then he turned back. "May I ask why you're back so soon, General?"

"The Grand Master wasn't home, according to his assistants," Nikki responded, sounding irritated. "And then I return to this... this debacle. I think drilling the men might be in order, captain. Have the men fall in immediately."

"Yes, General!"

Captain Edmond called the men to order. The weapons of Nikki's companions were stacked to one side, and the soldiers quickly formed ranks—five rows of ten men each.

"I wish to inspect the men, Captain," Nikki said. She proceeded to walk smartly between each row of soldiers, while her companions quietly moved closer to their weapons.

Once Nikki had finished her inspection, she said, "Captain, your men seem soft. Softer than the soldiers I command in the field. Why is that?"

"I cannot say, General," the captain responded. "We follow the same daily training as the rest of the army."

"Did you follow that training this morning?"

"No, General. The men were deployed well before sunrise. There was no time."

"There's time now, Captain. We're strangers in a strange and inhospitable land. The spear must be sharp or we could perish here, unburied, unremembered, unsung. Your men are our spear, and they must be sharp. Carry out the morning exercises and training immediately."

"Yes, General!"

Nikki stepped back, fighting the urge to laugh. Her time in the army had prepared her for her performance, but being mistaken for a general and a Princess made her feel powerful, and it was like nothing she had ever felt before. She was enjoying herself, but she was mindful of the next phase of the plan, and she watched the road closely for the appearance of Atreus.

She gestured for her companions to recover their weapons and stand aside.

As the soldiers began their morning training, she heard a galloping horse approaching the barracks. *Showtime.*

She saw Atreus, disguised as Princess Angélique, riding toward the soldiers.

"Treachery!" Nikki shouted. She pointed at Atreus. "Imposter! What's going on here, Captain? Who is this person pretending to be me?"

Atreus leaped from his saddle and strode toward the captain. "Captain, can't you see that this person is the *real* imposter? Seize her. Now!"

Captain Edmond, and most of his soldiers, looked at the two Princess Angéliques standing in front of them. "Which one of you is the real one?" he muttered.

Nikki pointed to Atreus. "This is the imposter, Captain." She drew her sword, and before Atreus could react, she struck him with the flat part of her sword blade. At the same time, she concentrated, forcing the shapeshifter back into his true form. Atreus appeared, leaving Nikki as the only Princess Angélique in the presence of the soldiers.

"Atreus-the-shapeshifter!" the captain exclaimed.

"You know this man?" Nikki demanded.

The captain nodded. "He's one of your sister's... favorites, in a manner of speaking."

"I get the idea, Captain," Nikki said. "Seize him!"

Four soldiers rushed forward and grabbed Atreus. He tried to shapeshift, but Nikki pressed the point of her sword against his chest while forcing him back into his real form. Atreus looked confused and then terrified when he realized that he couldn't shapeshift anymore.

"Who did this to me?" he demanded, trembling. "Is this the Grand Master's doing?"

Nikki smiled and glanced at Justin and Livvy, who both nodded. She withdrew her sword, and before Atreus could react, Nikki struck him in the face.

Livvy immediately placed Atreus into an unconscious state while Justin made certain that Atreus couldn't change form again.

"Captain, if he's a shapeshifter, then it's going to be hard to keep him in custody. He could transform into another form and escape. He needs to be kept unconscious until we can return him to the portal. If he appears to be regaining consciousness, someone needs to knock him out again."

"Yes, General," the captain promised. Then he cocked

his head to one side. "The portal, General?"

Nikki nodded. "Yes, Captain. There's more going on here than I was led to believe. This man proves it. I think the Grand Master should decide his fate. I need you to take your men back to the Realm of the High Kingdom. Demand an audience with the King, my sister, the nobles, and our Portal Keeper. Tell them everything that has happened."

"What about you, General?"

"I need to get back to the army, Captain. I left in the middle of a campaign, and they need me. I'll have the Grand Master send me to my army's camp after you and your men are safely back in the High Kingdom."

"Yes, General."

The captain looked at Nikki's companions. "And what of the prisoners?"

"Release them," Nikki said. "I don't know what Atreus wanted them for, but I'm not going to allow one of his plans to go any farther. Any objections, Captain?"

"No, General."

"Good. Have your men retrieve their supplies and horses. We ride for the portal in ten minutes."

"Yes, General."

The captain shouted orders, and the men broke ranks to carry them out.

Nikki's companions walked toward her. "Nicely done, *General*," Justin whispered. "If I didn't know better, I'd bet you were Princess Angélique."

"I could get used to this," Nikki said, smiling. Turning to Livvy, she asked, "Do you have Atreus under your control?"

Livvy nodded. "He's out cold and will remain that way

until I release him."

A few minutes later, the soldiers were mounted and waiting for Nikki's orders.

"We ride directly for the portal," Nikki shouted. "Half of you take the point. Captain, you will accompany me behind the vanguard, along with the captives and the prisoner. The remaining soldiers bring up the rear."

"Yes, General." The captain issued the orders, and the soldiers started riding west toward the portal.

Livvy communicated with Thor to let him know they were returning and that the plan had worked perfectly. He promised that he'd be waiting for them at the portal.

"It's all set," Livvy whispered to Nikki. "Are you sure you want to go through with the last part of the plan?"

Nikki nodded. "Damn right, I do."

"Okay. Just making sure."

They made good time back to the portal, arriving before sunset. Thor was there with his assistants, waiting for them.

"Greetings, Grand Master," Nikki said formally when the soldiers stopped and allowed her to move to the front of the column.

"Greetings, Princess Angélique," Thor responded, hiding his amusement. "I see you brought a few soldiers with you."

"Not me, Grand Master. This imposter brought them." Nikki gestured toward Atreus, who was still unconscious. "He impersonated me and conned these good soldiers into coming here with him to carry out whatever plans he had for you and your portal."

Thor nodded solemnly. "What is your wish, Princess?"

"Send the soldiers back to the Realm of the High Kingdom. They need to report to the King and tell him what has happened. Then, if you'd be so kind, would you send me back to my army?"

"Of course, Princess." Thor pointed to Atreus. "And what of him?"

Nikki smiled. "I leave that entirely up to you."

"Very well." Thor opened the portal to the Realm of the High Kingdom. "Captain, if you all will dismount and lead your horses through, you may enter the portal."

The captain complied, as did his men. "Thank you, Grand Master. And please accept my apology and the apoologies of my men for invading your lands. Our presence here was... unfortunate."

"Think nothing of it, Captain."

The captain turned to Nikki, who dismounted and faced him. "General, thank you for keeping us from making a grave mistake. It is an honor to be in your service."

"Do something for me, Captain," Nikki said softly so only he could hear it.

"Anything, General."

"Keep an eye on my sister," Nikki said. "There's something going on, and she's part of it. I want her watched closely, and whenever possible, pass that information along to the Grand Master."

The captain nodded. "I will, General." He saluted her. "Until we meet again."

"Until then, Captain." Nikki returned the salute.

The captain led his horse into the portal, followed by the rest of his men.

The Portal of Alesia

Once all of the soldiers were through the portal, Thor closed it behind him.

"I'm glad that's over," he said. "That was good thinking, Nikki, asking him to watch Princess Telise. I'd like to know what she's up to, since it clearly involves trying to gain control of the portals."

"I thought you'd like that," Nikki said.

"Time to deal with Atreus," Livvy said. "Is everyone ready?"

"Ready," Justin confirmed.

"Ready," Nikki confirmed.

"Ready," Thor confirmed.

"Okay," Livvy said. She concentrated for a moment, and Atreus started stirring. Kevin and Justin hauled Atreus to his feet and held onto him while Justin also stood ready to transform Atreus back into his true form if he tried to shapeshift again.

Thor and Nikki stood in front of Atreus. When his eyes opened, he saw the two of them. His face went white when he saw Princess Angélique glaring at him.

"Your Royal Highness, I can explain."

"There is nothing you could explain that I don't already know," Nikki said with as much contempt as she could put into her voice. "You conspired with my sister to take control of the master portal, you tricked my soldiers into coming here and capturing these good people, and you planned to murder them until the Grand Master agreed to your demands. Is there anything else you want to explain to me?"

"It was your sister, Telise, who was behind everything," Atreus said quickly. "I simply did her bidding."

"As well as servicing her in bed like a common prostitute," Nikki spat. "You're despicable. Yes, I know my sister is involved, but the lengths you were willing to go to are what leaves you condemned."

Thor opened the portal. What lay on the other side was unrecognizable. "What is that place?" Atreus demanded.

"One of the worlds my predecessor explored," Thor said. "In fact, it's the last world he explored before you caused his death, Atreus. It's an inhospitable place. Nine tenths of the surface is covered in water. There are no land animals and little vegetation. There are a few birds, but the waters are filled with fish. If you're strong and quick, you just might survive."

Fear filled Atreus. "That's where you're sending me?"

"You prefer death to exile?" Thor asked.

"Or torture, perhaps?" Nikki asked. She nodded to Livvy, who returned her to her normal form. "Recognize me, Atreus?"

Atreus' eyes bugged out when he saw Nikki. "You! The... warrior girl. But... but... you're dead! I saw you after my men tortured you. How are you here?" His knees nearly buckled, but Kevin and Justin kept him upright. "Wait. You're the reason I can't shapeshift?"

"One of the reasons, Atreus," Nikki stated with as much contempt as she could convey with her voice. "Three of us, not counting the Grand Master, have the ability to force a shapeshifter back into his true form. I guess that never occurred to you. And I wasn't dead, but I nearly was. I got better, no thanks to you. But I'd be happy to do to you what your men did to me, if you'd find that preferable to a fish diet for the rest of your life."

The Portal of Alesia

Atreus trembled. "No, I'll take exile."

He tried one last time to shapeshift and escape, but Nikki, Livvy, and Justin prevented him. He finally gave up.

Nikki handed her sword and dagger to Kevin. Then she picked up Atreus in a fireman's carry and marched toward the portal. As she stood before the opening, she shifted her grip, grabbing him by his collar and his belt, facing the ground. She began to swing him, building up momentum. Then she released him, and he flew through the portal to the world of his exile. Nikki watched him land and roll away. Then the portal closed, and Atreus was gone.

"What kind of fish are on that world?" Kevin asked.

"They're all carnivorous," Thor said, laughing. "The tamest fish on that planet are similar to piranha and sharks. If he even touches the water to catch one, they'll eat him alive before he knows that happened to him."

Bethany's hands flew up to her mouth. "Thor! That's gruesome."

"But fitting for his crimes," Thor said, putting his arm around Bethany's waist. "He was willing to kill all of us to gain control of the portal. It's only proper that the portal decide his fate. I didn't select that world, but I recognized it immediately from the memories that my predecessor gave me. If that's where the portal wanted him to go, then that's where he was destined to go."

"It's always destiny where the portals are concerned," Bethany accused.

"Yes, it is," Thor replied. "I know it's hard to understand, but that's the honest truth. I didn't make it that way, but I'm bound to it. I'm sorry if that bothers you."

Bethany just shook her head and said nothing.

"So what happens now?" Kevin asked.

"We eat supper," Thor said.

Kevin laughed. "No, I mean after that."

"I need to summon a council of Portal Keepers and inform them what happened. I need to meet with Essien, who's the Portal Keeper in the High Kingdom, and let him know that he needs to choose his successor immediately. And I need to meet with his successor so he knows not to fall for the schemes of King Constantine or Princess Telise. After that, I guess it'll be time for all of you to return home. This quest is finished."

Hearing Thor state that the quest was finished put the companions in a strange mood as they walked up the road to the Grand Master's residence. This wouldn't be like the end of their last quest. This time, they were leaving one behind, and the reality of that suddenly hit all of them—Bethany the hardest.

Chapter 13

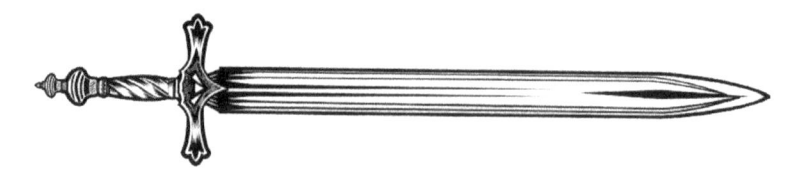

Dinner that night was a sad affair. The quest was over, but they were losing one of their team members forever—possibly two, depending on what Bethany finally decided.

After dinner, the men retired to the library. Thor wanted to discuss how to have his affairs on Earth settled without him being there to help.

"I'll write out my resignation to the university and my notice of move out from my apartment," Thor said, "but I'll need all of my things packed up and put in storage or sold."

"If you're never coming back, why put them in storage?" Peter asked. "Shouldn't we just sell them or consign them somewhere and be done with it?"

"If the three of you don't mind handling that for me," Thor responded. "I want this to be as painless for all of you as possible. There's so much to do. My final bills have to be paid, my accounts closed, utilities shut off... It's a long list."

"We'll get it done for you," Kevin promised.

"What do you want done with the proceeds from the sale and the balance in your bank account?" Justin asked.

Thor responded. "I want it donated to that program you started, the one where you use climbing as a way to help vets with PTSD. Put it all there."

"Are you sure?" Justin asked.

Thor nodded. "Use it to help people who need the help. I trust you to use it properly... and wisely."

Justin promised to take care of the funds so they weren't wasted.

Peter leaned forward with a pained look on his face. "I can't believe you're really staying here. We've been the four musketeers for so long. But that's over now, isn't it?"

"It is," Thor confirmed. "And I'll miss all of you, but this is where I'm supposed to be, doing what I'm supposed to do. I have to stay, and the three of you have to go. You have lives that need living, and you have girlfriends that need loving. Build new lives with them and never look back. There's another adventure waiting for you that's better than just four guys hanging out together every week. It's time to move on. I'll miss all of you, but if you're living better lives, I'll be happy."

"And what about Bethany?" Kevin asked.

Thor took a deep breath and let it out slowly. "I've asked her to stay with me. She's still thinking about it. I imagine the girls are talking about it now, giving her plenty of advice."

Thor was correct.

Nikki, Livvy, Allison, and Bethany were in the parlor,

down the hall from the library, talking to Bethany about her plans for the future.

"He really asked you to stay?" Allison asked.

Bethany nodded. "Part of me wants to, and part of me doesn't want to. It's a big decision."

"Is it?" Livvy asked. "There's a life with Thor, here, and there's a life back home. There's new things to see and do here, and there's your old job back home... a job that has been promising you a promotion for, what, two years now but has yet to deliver on that promise? Frankly, I'm beginning to think that they're just promising it to get you to work yourself to death and then burn out so they don't have to promote you."

Bethany's eyes opened wide, and then she glared at Livvy. "How could you even suggest that the hospital is using me like that?" she demanded.

"Because the hospital is using you like that," Allison stated. "If they planned to promote you, they would have done it already. The fact that they haven't, even though you've more than earned it, shows that they don't plan to ever give it to you. Face it, you're too valuable where you are to promote. They could never replace you."

Nikki joined the discussion. "So if you go home and demand that promotion, they might finally give you the job that should have been yours two years ago. And if they don't give it to you, or if they promise that you'll be getting it soon but won't commit to a date, I don't see why you'd be willing to stay in your current position, killing yourself for a promise when they haven't kept their promises to you. So, you'll either get promoted, or you'll quit and go to a hospital that'll treat you better, but either way, the hospital will have to replace you, which is clearly something they don't want to do. But if you stay here, they'll have to replace you anyway. So no matter what, the hospital will have to replace you. It's just a matter of where you'll be going—a new position at your current hospital, a new job at a different hospital, or a new life here with Thor. No matter what happens, your life is going to change, so if it's the fear of change that's keeping you from making your decision, you can forget about that, since change is coming. All that remains is to decide which change you want the most—new position, new job, or new life."

"And how do you know that I won't be happy keeping my current job at the hospital?" Bethany demanded.

"Because you're better than that job," Allison answered. "And you hate being lied to; all they've done *for years* is lie you about that damn promotion. You love the work, but you can't keep working for a hospital that doesn't value *you*. All they care about is what they can get *from* you. And it isn't costing them anything to make you work harder... just a promise that they don't intend to keep."

Bethany shifted in her seat and took a sip of wine that one of Thor's assistants had brought to the parlor. She held the goblet, rubbing it with her hand. "So if I leave here, there's a lot of change waiting for me at home."

"Exactly," Nikki said.

"Well, what if I did stay?" Bethany asked. "What happens to all of my things?"

"We can handle that for you," Livvy said. "I imagine Thor is either gonna have the guys sell his things or put them in storage. We can do the same with yours. Just write out a letter of resignation to the hospital, sign another letter that tells the landlord you're moving out, and let one of us get onto your computer to pay your bills and close

The Portal of Alesia

your accounts. All we need then is to know what to do with the money in your account."

"You make it sound so easy," Bethany said.

"It is, if you let us help you," Nikki said. "You're not alone, you know. We're here for you, even if we're half a universe away. That'll never change."

Allison stared at Bethany, who was clearly paralyzed by the decision she was facing. "I think there's something we're overlooking here. Bethany, do you love Thor?"

"With all my heart," Bethany replied.

"Then are you willing to give up your old life to be with him, just like he's had to give up his old life? Do you want to build a new life together or don't you?"

"It's not the same," Bethany retorted. "Thor didn't give up his old life for me."

"Oh, yes he did," Livvy stated. "He most certainly did. He sacrificed himself so we could all go back home, if that's what we wanted to do. That includes you. He wants you to stay. That's obvious. But he has given you the ability to choose your future, and that's a gift. He could have refused to become Grand Master, forcing all of us to remain here forever, but he didn't. Are you willing to sacrifice, too? Give up what you have back home and build something new, here, with the man you love? That's the question. That's the issue that needs to be resolved. What to do with your stuff is hardly important compared to the question you need to answer."

Bethany nodded her head, but she said nothing. She was lost in her thoughts, unable to choose between the paths facing her.

The next morning, Essien arrived through the portal, along with one of his assistants named Goff. Thor met them at the portal and spoke to them there.

"Are you aware that you allowed the shapeshifter Atreus back through the portal with 50 soldiers from the Realm of the High Kingdom?" Thor demanded of Essien.

Essien hung his head. "I became aware of this when the soldiers returned and demanded an audience with the King and his nobles, Grand Master. I was summoned, and I was informed about what had happened. Atreus impersonated Princess Angélique, and I was duped into opening the portal for him."

"After I had warned you about allowing anyone to travel here without a thorough investigation first to confirm the legitimacy of the request?"

Essien nodded.

"And did you investigate the legitimacy of the request?"

"Grand Master, it was Princess Angélique, or at least I thought it was. Why would I doubt her? Why wouldn't I honor her request?"

"Because she was bringing fifty soldiers here in the dead of night!" Thor roared. "That didn't make you suspicious?"

Essien stood in silence.

Thor shook his head in disgust. "Now I have to decide what to do. Part of me wants to close the portal in the High Kingdom so it can never be used to send people or soldiers anywhere ever again."

Essien looked at Thor, eyes wide. "You... you can't, Grand Master! How will the High Kingdom remain the

The Portal of Alesia

High Kingdom if it can't send soldiers to the other realms or receive tribute? The Eight Realms would no longer exist as they do today."

"And that's a bad thing, Essien? Someone in the High Kingdom wants control of the portals, something we have all sworn to prevent, and yet you acquiesce to every request the High Kingdom makes of you, even when it puts the Portal of Alesia at risk, the Grand Master at risk, and the rest of the portals at risk. If I isolated the High Kingdom, all of their intrigues will fail, and the other realms will be free to decide if they still need a single leader or if they're better off on their own."

Essien began trembling.

"Your reaction to my suggestion tells me that you're a supporter of those intrigues, Essien," Thor accused. "For that reason, you can no longer remain a Portal Keeper."

Thor turned to Goff. "Is Goff your successor?"

"Yes, Grand Master," Essien said darkly.

"Has the Portal of the High Kingdom accepted him?"

"Yes, Grand Master."

"Then transfer your power and knowledge to him. Now."

"What?"

"Now, Essien. You are stripped of your portal. It will no longer respond to you. Now complete the transfer."

Essien faced Goff and placed his hands on either side of Goff's head. He closed his eyes. A few minutes later, his eyes opened, and he lowered his arms. "It is done, Grand Master."

Thor looked at Goff. "Did you receive Essien's knowledge and power?"

Goff nodded. "Yes, Grand Master."

"Good. Return to the High Kingdom and complete the bonding with your portal. Once that is completed, return here."

"Yes, Grand Master."

Thor opened the portal, and Goff disappeared through it. When the portal was closed, Thor looked at Essien.

"Now I have to decide what to do with you," he growled.

"What did you do to Atreus?" Essien asked.

"He was banished to another world," Thor replied. "One that is mostly water. I imagine he's been eaten by now, and if not... well... it's just a matter of time."

Essien began trembling again. "Is that the fate you have in store for me?"

Thor stared at the powerless man. "No, but I can't have you return to the High Kingdom and reveal our secrets, either. There has been too much of that already. You will be banished, but where on this world can I send you where you won't get into any mischief? Do I have to exile you to another world?"

Thor closed his eyes and communed with the portal. Then he had the answer he sought.

"The portal doesn't trust you to remain on this world, so it has selected another world for you." The portal opened, showing a tropical world that had been discovered and explored several hundred years earlier.

"This world has abundant plant life, food, and land and water animals. The weather is mild, but there are no humans. You will be alone, but your needs can be met, with a little ingenuity and determination on your part."

Essien looked through the portal and then back to Thor. "You expect me to go there for the rest of my life?"

The Portal of Alesia

"I could send you where I sent Atreus," Thor pointed out. "It's your choice... an excellent opportunity for life, or certain death."

Essien looked at the portal again. "I choose life."

"Then enter the portal and begin your exile."

Essien complied, and Thor closed the portal after him.

A moment later, Goff returned through the portal. He looked around. "Where is Essien?"

"My portal has exiled him to another world, but don't worry. He has everything there he needs for a long life."

Goff nodded.

"Do you understand what I expect of you as Portal Keeper?" Thor asked.

Goff nodded.

"And you understand what I demand of you regarding your interactions with the monarchy, nobility, and military of the Realm of the High Kingdom?"

"None of them are to be allowed to come here, and I'm to prevent any attempts to learn about the portals or control the portals, even if it means sacrificing myself for my portal."

"That is correct. No one but you or your successor may travel here through your portal without my expressed permission. If anyone other than you or your successor travels here through your portal without my permission, I'll close your portal. Forever."

"Yes, Grand Master."

The other Portal Keepers arrived a few minutes later, in answer to Thor's summons. He brought them up to speed on Atreus' latest attempt to seize the portal and Princess Telise's potential involvement. He then introduced them to Goff and told the others that Goff was Essien's successor.

"And where is Essien now?" Ravana, the tavern owner, asked.

"He has been exiled to another world," Thor replied. "As has Atreus, as will anyone who tries to take control of the portals, as will any Portal Keeper who aides in taking control of the portals. Keeping the portals safe and independent from any monarch, noble, or soldier is our principal responsibility, and now that we have been betrayed by one of our own, even a tacit betrayal, the punishments will be much harsher to prevent it from happening again. There is too much intrigue going on in the Realm of the High Kingdom, and we must all be vigilant. There's more going on than just trying to seize the portals, but the portals clearly play a part in their plans. We must stay in close contact so we can react to whatever happens before disaster occurs."

The Portal Keepers all agreed, and then they returned to their portals.

Ravana remained behind for a few minutes. He looked up toward the residence. "When are your fellow questers returning to their homes, Grand Master?"

"Tomorrow or the next day," Thor replied. "I'll let you know once they've decided."

"I'll be ready, Grand Master."

Thor walked up to the residence and saw his fellow questers watching him from the front porch.

The Portal of Alesia

"All finished with your meetings?" Justin asked.

Thor nodded. "The Portal Keeper from the Realm of the High Kingdom has transferred his power to his successor and has been banished. The new Portal Keeper has been given instruction about what he is and is not allowed to do where Alesia is concerned, and the other Portal Keepers were informed about what Atreus did and what we're going to do to help prevent intrigues from tearing the realms apart, even if it means closing the portal in the High Kingdom forever."

"Sounds like you're preparing for war," Livvy said.

"The realms are, and we must respond. After all, it's hard to move troops from one realm to the other without using the portals. It will be up to us to ensure the stability and peace of the realms in case the intrigues get out of hand."

"What did the tavern owner ask you before he left?" Nikki asked.

"When you were all heading home," Thor replied. "I told him I'd let him know once you made your decision."

That night, Thor and Bethany stayed up and talked for most of the night in their chamber.

"So you've made your decision?" Thor asked once the conversation had run its course.

Bethany nodded. "I'm going home with the others. There's a lot that I need to do. People at the hospital that I need to confront."

"I'll miss you," Thor said.

Bethany brushed a tear from her cheek with the back

of her hand. "I'll miss you, too, Thor, but we both know that this is something I have to do."

Thor nodded. Then he reached for her and pulled her close. "I love you, you know."

"And I love you," Bethany responded.

Knowing that this was their last night, they spent the rest of it making love until the first morning light streamed through the window.

When they came downstairs, the other questers were waiting for them. They all stared at each other, and then Thor hugged each of them one at a time.

When he came to Nikki, he whispered, "I'm happy to see you fully recovered. You've been through so much since I first met you at the tavern, and you've proven yourself to be the most resilient person I've ever known. I know only great things are in store for you."

Nikki kissed him. She was too choked up to say anything, and tears were streaming down her face. He released her, and she stepped back with the others. Then Thor led them down to the portal.

Before he opened the portal to the tavern at Riverstone, Thor said, "If you ever need to reach me, you can get a message to me via Ravana and the game. If I need to reach you, I'll do it the same way."

Thor looked at Bethany, and then he hugged and kissed her again. Neither said a word. All that needed to be said had been said already.

Thor opened the portal, and they saw the tavern appear. The tavern owner waved a greeting to them.

Justin and Nikki looked at each other, looked at Thor, and then looked at the others. They nodded to Thor and led the others through the portal. Once everyone was in the

The Portal of Alesia

tavern, Thor closed the portal behind them.

"Welcome back, courageous questers," the tavern owner said when they arrived and the portal had closed. "It's good to see you again, but I imagine this is a sadder departure than before."

Bethany nodded.

"Are you all ready to return home?"

Nikki and Justin both said, "Yes."

"Very well. Until we meet again."

They heard the familiar rumble of thunder. Then there was a bright flash of white light.

Returning Home

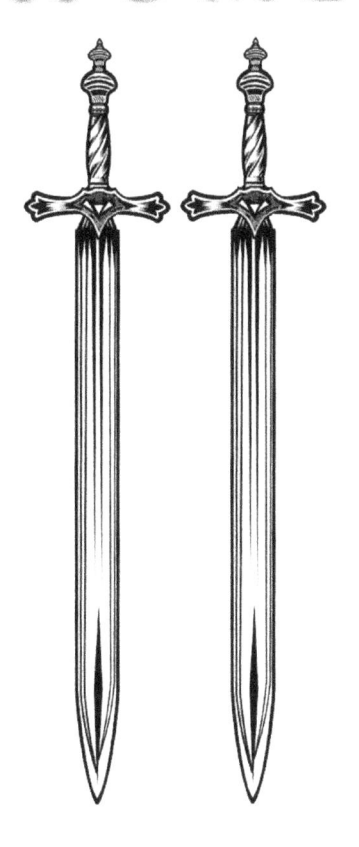

Chapter 14

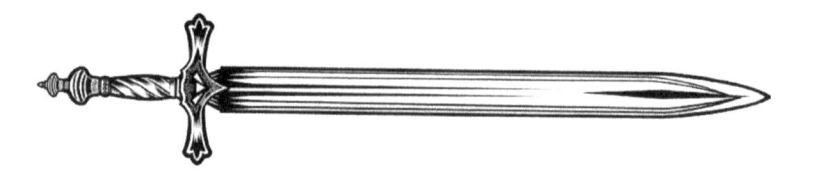

Nikki looked around at the inside of her apartment. Everyone was sitting exactly where they had been before they agreed to go on the quest... everyone except Thor. His spot on the couch was empty.

The tavern owner was on the TV screen looking at them. "Be safe, my friends," he said.

Nikki nodded, and then she turned off the game controller. The TV screen went blank.

Bethany looked at Thor's empty spot next to her. She stood and left the apartment.

"Bethany..." Allison called after her.

Bethany didn't return.

"I'll check on her in the morning," Allison said.

"*We'll* check on her in the morning," Livvy corrected. She stood and looked around. "I'm heading home. I'll talk to y'all in the morning."

"I'll walk you home," Kevin said, rising to his feet.

"I live across the hall," Livvy reminded him.

"I'll walk you home anyway." He looked around and added, "Good night, y'all. Talk soon."

Livvy and Kevin left.

Allison and Peter left next.

"I'll help you clean up," Justin offered, grabbing empty glasses and plates off the coffee table.

Nikki stood and started putting away the food. As Justin joined her in the kitchen, he saw her calendar posted on the refrigerator door.

"Are you going to the RenFaire next weekend?" he asked, tapping the notation on the calendar.

Nikki nodded. "I'm working my uncle's blacksmith shop. Livvy and Bethany are supposed to be there to help, but I don't know if they're still planning to attend. I think Allison and Peter are going away this coming weekend, but I'll be there this weekend and the next weekend, definitely."

"I'll be there, too," Justin said. "Several of my students will be performing in the joust and tests of arms, and I've been asked to be one of the referees."

Nikki smiled. "Want to go together?"

"I'd love to," Justin said. Then a strange look crossed his face. "It'll be strange wearing armor in this world for a change."

"At least no one will be trying to kill us," Nikki noted as she put the food away.

When the food was all put away, Nikki asked, "Can you stay the night?"

Justin nodded.

Nikki put her hand up and motioned toward the couch. "I want to talk, first."

"Okay." Curious, he followed her to the couch and sat

The Portal of Alesia

next to her. She curled up next to him.

"What's going to happen with Thor's things here?" Nikki asked.

"We're going to sell it all," Justin replied. "It's what he wants."

"And what about Bethany?"

"I was going to ask you that," Justin said. "I was surprised that she came back with us, and I'm surprised that Thor wasn't more broken up about it."

"Me, too," Nikki confided. "There's something up between them, but I don't know what it is."

"You talked to her?"

"Not since she and Thor talked last night," she replied. "I have no idea what they decided, but she did come back with us. Read into that what you want."

They talked for a while longer, and then Nikki asked, "Are we good?"

"Of course we are," Justin replied, pulling her close. "I think we're closer than ever. We've proven that we have each other's backs when it comes to combat. Now we need to focus on being together and having fun. The RenFaire should be a blast!"

"You know what they say about RenFaires, don't you?" Nikki asked coyly.

Justin shook his head.

"If you can't get laid at a RenFaire, you can't get laid anywhere," Nikki said.

Justin laughed.

Nikki uncurled herself and stood. "Speaking of which, I need a shower." She reached out her hand. "Care to join me?"

Justin didn't need to be asked twice.

Monday morning, Bethany got ready for work several hours earlier than the start of her shift. She had a meeting with her boss and the head of human resources that morning, and she didn't want to be late.

She had managed to keep from seeing her friends the day before, having a number of errands she needed to run that took most of the day. She navigated through the boxes in her apartment to reach the front door, and then she headed for the hospital.

Her purse contained a letter that she had spent several hours writing the night before. She was pleased with it, but she was anxious about presenting it to the folks she was meeting with that morning.

She arrived at the hospital five minutes early and was ushered into the HR Director's office. Her boss arrived two minutes later.

"What did you want to talk about, Bethany?" her boss said when she sat down.

"This phantom promotion that you've been dangling in front of my face for two years," Bethany responded.

"What do you mean by 'phantom'?" the HR Director asked.

"For two years, I've been told that I'm getting the promotion to Head Surgical Nurse. It hasn't happened. I've done all the work requested, I've put in all the overtime requested, I've done everything I was told would speed up the process, and I still don't have the promotion. I don't believe there is a promotion. I believe the position doesn't exist, and I believe I've been lied to for two years with the

The Portal of Alesia

offer of a promotion just to make me work myself to death for the same pay I've been receiving all along. Well, I'm tired of being lied to. I want the honest truth. Is there a promotion, am I getting it, and if so, when *exactly* am I getting it? I want an exact date."

Both the HR Director and Bethany's boss looked uncomfortable and started squirming in their seats. Bethany knew in that moment that they had been lying to her, and they were both in on the lie.

"Look, Bethany," the HR Director said. "We don't want to lose you—"

"I don't work with or for people I can't trust," Bethany interrupted. "If this is how you show your support for your best employees, as you've called me a number of times, then I can't work at this hospital any longer. No promotion or raise for two years after it was promised to me time after time after time? No. I'm done. Find another fool to lie to. I'm out of here."

Bethany took the letter from her purse and flung it at the HR Director. "My letter of resignation, effective immediately."

"We require a month's notice," Bethany's boss said automatically.

"So what?" Bethany snapped. "I don't need a reference from this place, you can't legally hold my final check, and you've been committing a fraud on me for two years. Be glad I don't take legal action against you. You will pay me my final check, and you will pay out my unused vacation time with no penalties for lack of notice. Is that clear?"

The HR Director and Bethany's boss were both stunned by her forcefulness. Realizing that there was no way to repair the damage, they simply nodded.

"Good." Bethany stood. "I want it deposited in my account by end of day tomorrow, as required by state law. And it had all better be there."

She removed her lanyard with her identification cards on it. She dropped it on the desk, along with her keys. "I'm going to empty my locker now, and then I'm leaving the building for the last time. I hope you don't pull this on any more nurses here. It would be a shame if we all took it to the board as a pattern of workplace abuse in this place."

With that, Bethany exited the office. She went to her locker on the fourth floor, which was filled mostly with spare nurses' uniforms and shoes. She tossed it all away, grabbed the two sweaters she kept in the locker, along with an umbrella, slammed her locker shut, and left the hospital, feeling free for the first time in ages.

"One down, two to go."

On Saturday morning, Nikki and Justin arrived at the RenFaire, just outside of town, two hours before opening. They both parked their cars in the staff parking lot. Then they began unloading all of their gear, costumes, and equipment.

Once inside the faire grounds, Nikki gave Justin a kiss, and they headed in different directions—Justin toward the jousting arena, and Nikki toward her uncle's blacksmith shop. She heard the familiar clanging of hammer on steel as she approached the booth.

"Hi, Nikki," one of her uncle's assistants called out.

"Hi, Fred," Nikki called back. "Hi, Uncle David!"

Uncle David looked up from the metal bar he was

flattening. "Hi, sweetheart! Glad you're here. Are your friends coming?"

"Livvy is, Allison isn't, and I have no idea about Bethany. She's gone radio-silent on us for some reason."

Nikki pulled all of her things into the booth and started getting dressed. She gave Uncle David a kiss, and added, "My boyfriend Justin is working with the jousters, but he's coming by later, as is Livvy's boyfriend, who's Justin's boss."

"I can't wait to meet them," Uncle David said. "You've been glowing for the past few weeks, so it'll be good to see the person partly responsible for that."

Livvy showed up with Kevin about thirty minutes later. She was already in her RenFaire outfit. Kevin was wearing street clothes, but Livvy promised that he'd be fully outfitted by the end of the weekend.

Justin dropped by several times, and he and Nikki had the chance to walk around together and see some of the shows.

"So Bethany's a no-show?" Justin asked after they had finished lunch.

"So it seems. No one's heard from her all week."

"And where are Allison and Peter?" he asked.

"Florida, for a long weekend getaway. I have no idea what they're planning next weekend."

"At least you, me, Livvy, and Kevin will all be here next weekend."

Nikki smiled. "As long as you and I are together, that's all that really matters to me."

Justin looked around and then stole a kiss from Nikki. "Do you want to put what you said about RenFaires to the test later?"

"In the privacy of your or my apartment? Yes. Here at the faire grounds? Not a chance. I have no desire to make love on the ground, in a tent, or in the back seat of a car. Our beds are less than twenty minutes away. That's all the 'roughing it' I'm willing to do."

"Sounds perfect to me."

Bethany spent the days leading up to the weekend packing her things into boxes, and taking those boxes over to Thor's apartment. The guys had already started boxing his things to get them ready for the consignment shop that was going to sell it all, and she added her boxes to the stacks.

There was nothing she could do about her furniture, but she had written instructions that she'd leave with her friends regarding what to do with anything she left behind.

She was able to get most of her things packed and moved to Thor's apartment before everyone returned Sunday night. What remained would last her the week, and then it would be added to the boxes at Thor's apartment.

Sunday night, Nikki and Justin arrived at his apartment. Nikki helped him get all of his gear back upstairs and put away. They had grabbed a couple of deli sandwiches on the way, and they ate them ravenously. Between the physical exertion, and having to wear armor in the hot sun for two days, they were starving, they were thirsty, and they were unbelievably horny.

After dinner, and a couple of beers, Nikki joined

The Portal of Alesia

Justin in his shower. Hers was larger, but the size of his shower made bathing and sex more fun. It didn't take long before Nikki had her arms around his neck and her legs around his waist as he thrust while clutching her butt. He had her back against the tiles of the back wall of his shower, while the water cascaded along their skin.

Nikki gasped each time Justin lowered her, causing his erection to penetrate deeper. She clutched him tighter as she orgasmed, enjoying the feeling of his penetration, the skin on skin, and the water.

Justin came inside of her, and they quickly finished washing each other so they could dry themselves and continue in the bedroom.

As they walked into the bedroom, naked and holding hands, Nikki saw three beach towels at the foot of the bed, in addition to the hand towels on the night table. She knew what this meant.

She was right.

Justin spread the beach towels out and then gently pushed Nikki onto the bed. He kissed her, moved down to lick her nipples for a while, and then moved further down until his tongue was stimulating her clit. Using his fingers, he began stimulating her on the inside at the same time. As the stimulation intensified, she felt herself building to her own ejaculation. Suddenly, Justin moved his head away from her as her body began shaking uncontrollably. The orgasm hit her, and she squealed as she began squirting on the towels.

Justin didn't let up for a moment. He rapidly moved his hand back and forth across her clit, causing her to orgasm and squirt again. Nikki's squealing went up a full octave the second time as she bounced up and down from the gyrations of her muscles that she could no longer control. Tears streamed down her face, but it wasn't from pain, it was from the intensity of the pleasure that Justin was giving her.

Justin didn't stop.

The third time she orgasmed and squirted, Nikki nearly passed out from the intensity. Almost all of her muscles clenched, and she doubled over at her waist.

Justin was fully erect by this time, and Nikki pushed him onto his back and straddled him. He penetrated her immediately, enjoying the extra lubrication from her ejaculations. She slid up and down on top of him with virtually no resistance. After several minutes of his penetration, she pulled him out and squirted again, sending the spray onto his legs. He penetrated her again, and she began moving up and down faster than before.

In a quick move, he rolled her off of him until she was on her hands and knees. He penetrated her from behind, causing her to orgasm and squirt almost immediately. He pulled out until she was finished, and then he penetrated her again, grabbed her hips, and began moving her forward and backward on his erection.

Her next orgasm caused Nikki's knees to buckle. She fell flat on the bed, face down, panting to catch her breath.

Justin rolled her over and got on top of her, penetrating and thrusting deeply. Nikki wrapped her legs around him and locked her ankles together. Her arms were around his shoulders, and he couldn't pull out, even if he had wanted to. She rode him from underneath until he climaxed and she felt the warm liquid shooting deep inside of her. She squealed with delight from the sensation and clung to him even tighter.

The Portal of Alesia

"Good God, Justin! What you do to me!"

Justin smiled as he looked down at her angelic face. "What I do to you? What about what you do to me? No one has ever responded to me the way you do. It makes everything we do twice as intense. I may not cum as often as you do, but when I do, I see fireworks. God, the way you make me feel... it's... it's indescribable. I swear to you that I'll never make love to another woman again as long as I live. There's no one for me other than you—body, mind, and soul."

Nikki kissed him. "And if we never do this again?"

"There's still no one for me other than you," Justin stated confidently. "I don't care what we do. I care that we're doing it together."

Nikki looked at him intently. "I want to learn how to climb."

"You do?" Justin was surprised. Nikki had never mentioned having anything to do with the rock climbing center before, even though he had taken her firearms safety class and had been shooting with her several times.

Nikki nodded. "I want to help you with the work you do for vets."

"Why? Don't get me wrong, I'm thrilled you want to help, but what brought this on?"

"You helped me when no one else could. You saved me... from myself. I want to help you save others."

"Paying it forward?"

Nikki nodded. "That and spending more time with you while you're doing something you're truly passionate about. I don't have that many passions in my life. I closed myself off from them. Oh, I have friends and hobbies, but nothing that I can point to and know that I made a difference. I'd like to change that, and I'd like to do it with you, if you'll let me."

Justin beamed. "Of course, I'll let you. I think it's a wonderful idea."

Justin kissed her. He was still inside of her, and he felt his erection growing again.

Nikki smiled up at him. "I guess you want some more."

"Only if you do."

"I do."

On Friday evening, Nikki and Livvy were sitting on Nikki's couch, planning for the last weekend of the local RenFaire. They also shared how their relationships were going with Justin and Kevin.

Livvy was flabbergasted when Nikki described squirting and how Justin made it happen.

"I've got to teach Kevin about that," Livvy said. "Sounds like a blast."

"You have NO idea," Nikki confirmed. "No idea. But don't tell him where you found out about it."

Livvy glanced toward the door. "Is Bethany coming?"

"I invited her, but I haven't seen her since we got back from the tavern," Nikki said. "Neither has Allison."

"Not even at the hospital?"

Nikki shook her head. "I wish I knew what she's up to. I've even knocked on her door, but she doesn't answer."

The Portal of Alesia

The next morning, Kevin picked up Livvy for the RenFaire and followed Nikki to the faire grounds. Justin had just arrived at the staff parking lot, and the others pulled in next to him.

"Good morning," Nikki said cheerfully as she got out of her car.

"Good morning to you," Justin responded, giving her a kiss and a gentle squeeze of her butt.

They all grabbed their gear and costumes and headed inside. This would be the first weekend that Kevin would be in full costume, and Nikki was anxious to see what it looked like.

The day went well, and Uncle David's shop had more visitors than ever before. He sold out of everything that he'd premade for the weekend and had taken in quite a few custom orders.

An hour before closing, Allison and Peter ran up to the booth. "Bethany quit her job!" Allison exclaimed when she saw Nikki and Livvy.

"What! When?"

"The Monday after we got back from the last quest. She confronted her boss and HR, and then she quit on the spot. No notice, no nothing."

"We need to tell Justin and Kevin," Nikki said. "They're over at the jousting arena."

As they made their way to the jousting arena, Allison said, "There's more that I haven't told you. Bethany turned in the keys to her apartment this morning."

Nikki stopped dead in her tracks. She looked at the others, and then she sprinted to the jousting arena.

When she found Kevin and Justin, she was out of breath, but she managed to say, "Bethany... is going back...

to be with Thor."

"How do you know?" Kevin demanded.

"She quit her job last week, and she turned in the keys to her apartment this morning."

Kevin looked at Justin. "I told you there were more boxes in Thor's apartment than we packed."

Livvy, Allison, and Peter arrived, all out of breath from chasing Nikki.

"Why did you run away like that?" Livvy demanded.

"Because Bethany is going back to be with Thor," Nikki said.

"But how?" Allison asked. "She doesn't have a game console."

"No, but she has a key to my apartment," Nikki said.

They looked at each other for a moment, and then they raced for their cars.

"Please let us get there in time," Nikki said as she pulled out of the parking lot. Justin was sitting next to him, still wearing his full armor, as was Nikki. The rest of their gear and street clothes were still at the faire, and would remain there until tomorrow, when they went back for the last day.

"You really think she's going back?" Justin asked.

"It fits. She *really* hates goodbyes, she loves Thor, she quit her job, and she turned in her keys. Unless she's moving to Kansas, I think she's going to be with him."

They raced through weekend traffic and parked in their parking spaces below the apartment building. Then they caught the elevator to Nikki's floor.

When they arrived at Nikki's apartment, Bethany was there. A bottle of champagne was on the coffee table, and the tavern owner was on the TV screen.

The Portal of Alesia

"You got back sooner than expected," Bethany said, looking at her friends with a guilty expression on her face. She pointed to a stack of papers on the coffee table, along with keys and her wallet. "I left a note, along with instructions. I really wanted to be gone before you arrived. I've made my decision, and I didn't want to hear any of you try to talk me out of it."

"We know, but we'd never forgive you if you left without saying goodbye," Nikki said, stepping forward to give Bethany a hug.

The rest also stepped forward for a hug.

"Are you sure about this?" Livvy asked.

Bethany nodded. "More sure than anything in my life. Thor and I worked it all out on the last night we were there. I came back just long enough to settle my affairs. Now I'm going back... forever. Thor's waiting for me."

Allison wiped a tear from her eye. "So this is good—"

"Don't say it," Bethany said. "Don't anyone say it. We'll meet again, just over there instead of here. And who knows? We'll probably all be married by then and having kids. That's what normal people do."

"We're not normal," Justin reminded her.

Bethany smiled. "No, we're not."

"It's time to go, Bethany," the tavern owner said. "I need the rest of you courageous questers to step outside until she's here. Then you can say your goodbyes before I send her on to Alesia."

Everyone crowded around Bethany for a silent hug, and then they stepped outside into the hallway between Nikki's and Livvy's apartments. They heard the familiar thunder, and Nikki saw the bright white light flash underneath her door. They reentered her apartment, but

Bethany was gone.

They looked at the TV screen, and Bethany was there, standing next to the tavern owner. She was in her long hunter-green dress, and she looked happy to be back in the tavern again. The tavern owner pointed to the far wall, and the green oval of the portal appeared. Then they saw Thor waiting on the other side. He waved, and Nikki and the others waved back.

Bethany looked at Thor and then back to the others. "Be well, all of you."

"Be happy," Nikki said.

Bethany nodded and walked through the portal. The last thing they saw before the portal closed was Bethany in Thor's arms and Thor kissing her.

The tavern owner smiled as he looked at Nikki and the others. "She is where she belongs. She left some things for you on the table. She really did want to just slip away unnoticed."

"She almost did," Nikki said.

"I will miss you," the tavern owner said. "All of you. And should you return on some future quest, don't be surprised to find that your powers and skills have leveled up to the highest level possible on this world. A gift from the Grand Master. But that is for another time. So, until we meet again, I wish you well."

Before anyone could speak, the TV screen went blank, and the "Game Over" screen appeared. Nikki reached down and turned off the game console.

Livvy opened the champagne and poured everyone a glass. "To Bethany and Thor," she said, raising her glass. "May they find the happiness they so richly deserve."

Everyone drained their glasses.

The Portal of Alesia

Livvy distributed what was left in the bottle into the glasses.

"And here's to us," Nikki said. "We started as two teams of four, we became one team of eight, then we became four couples, and now there are three couples still here. May we all find joy and love as we move forward on our journeys."

Everyone raised and then drained the last of the champagne.

Then they looked at each other.

"So... what do we do now?"

"Is anyone hungry?" Livvy asked. "I've been dying to try some of the dishes we'll be serving at Kevin's Rock Climbing Center when the food service area opens next month. Anyone want a sneak peak at the menu?"

Everyone agreed.

Nikki looked at Justin, and she smiled. "I love you," she mouthed silently.

"I love you," he responded.

The End... Has Not Yet Been Reached

The Questers will Return in
The Final Quest.

About the Author

W. B. Speir is an Award-winning author. Born in Alabama, W. B. has lived in Michigan, Connecticut, Florida, and now resides in Texas. W. B. has 26 published novels, six of which are Royal Palm Literary Award Gold and Silver winners. W. B.'s novels span the Romance, Fantasy, Historical Fiction, Science Fiction, Espionage, Suspense, and Action-Adventure genres. *The Quester Trilogy* is W. B.'s first Romantasy series.

For more information about W. B., please visit the publisher's website at progressiverisingphoenix.com.

Progressive Rising Phoenix Press is an independent publisher. We offer wholesale pricing and multiple binding options with no minimum purchases for schools, libraries, book clubs, and retail vendors. We offer substantial discounts on bulk orders and discounts on individual sales through our online store. Please visit our website at:
www.ProgressiveRisingPhoenix.com

If you enjoyed reading this book, please review it on Amazon, B & N, or Goodreads. Thank you in advance!

Milton Keynes UK
Ingram Content Group UK Ltd.
UKHW032358250824
447288UK00001B/55